A Ghost Around the House

A GHOST
AROUND
THE HOUSE

WILLIAM MacKELLAR

illustrated by Marilyn Miller

SCHOLASTIC BOOK SERVICES
NEW YORK · TORONTO · LONDON · AUCKLAND · SYDNEY · TOKYO

Copyright © 1970 by William MacKellar.
This edition is published by Scholastic Book Services, a division of Scholastic Magazines, Inc., by arrangement with David McKay Company, Inc.

1st printing . . . . November 1972

Printed in the U.S.A.

FOR DAVID

who always did like ghosts

A Ghost Around the House

CHAPTER ONE

I GUESS, looking back, Halloween had something to do with it. I mean, if I hadn't been thinking about ghosts and goblins maybe I wouldn't have been snooping around Strowan Castle in the first place. And of course if I hadn't been poking around that eerie old mansion I would never have met Malcolm MacDhu, the two hundred and fifty year old ghost.

Not that everybody agreed, mind you, that Malcolm MacDhu was a ghost. Or for that matter that there even *was* a Malcolm MacDhu, ghost or no ghost. Only I know that there was someone with that name, that he did live in Strowan Castle and that he was a ghost. When you think about it, though, when do you get everybody to agree on anything? Mom says that's because we live in New England. Nobody agrees with anybody around here, which is why we are always having town meetings. Actually we live in a place called Litchville, just a short ways from Wethersfield, one of the oldest towns in Connecticut. Pop has a small joke that Wethersfield was a colonial village before there were any colonies. I mean Wethersfield is *old*.

Maybe this would be a good time to tell you about Pop. His name is Henry Trimble and he's a teacher. He's also a painter. Not a real painter like the kind who climb up ladders and paint houses. I mean the other kind—the ones who use skinny little brushes and like to paint apples lying on a table. That is, the apples lie on the table. Pop says I never explain things properly and I guess he's right.

Anyway, when Pop isn't painting apples he teaches Art Appreciation at Litchville Community College. I've never been able to figure out exactly what Art Appreciation is. There must be something to it, though, for it keeps Pop awfully busy. Twice a week he has classes at night for grown-ups who want to appreciate art too. I guess it isn't easy for some people to appreciate art.

Well, as I was saying, it all happened because it was around Halloween, the day before, to be exact. The windows in the shops along Main Street were all prettied up with hook-nosed witches riding on broomsticks, black cats and cut-outs of collapsible skeletons. It gave you a nice comfortable feeling to see them, scary and gruesome, glaring out at you from the other side of the windows, surrounded by huge stacks of orange and black Halloween candy.

I had been on my way home from school and after

leaving Main Street I suddenly got this crazy notion to swing east away from the village and go home by way of Dead Man's Swamp. Most days I don't go home that way. For one thing, it's longer and I'm usually in a hurry to get home after being cooped up in school all day. For another, if you go by way of Dead Man's Swamp you have to pass the ruins of Strowan Castle. And Strowan Castle with its blackened, crumbling walls, its gloomy windows and the weeds all around it, isn't exactly the most cheerful place on earth. As long as I can remember there have been stories in the village that Strowan Castle was haunted. Nobody seemed clear as to just what was haunting the old pile of weather-beaten rock on the edge of the swamp. Some old codgers claimed to have seen mysterious lights flickering there at night. When I told her Mom said it was probably kids lighting matches. Still, come to think of it none of the kids *I* know ever go to Strowan Castle at night. Or during the day for that matter.

I veered at Dead Man's Swamp and found the trail that led towards the castle. Although the marshland is an eerie enough place, nobody ever came across any dead bodies there that I know of and nobody is quite sure how it got its spooky name. Maybe it was just that if any dead body was to be found around Litchville, the swamp at the edge of the village was as good a place to find it as any.

I could see Strowan Castle now. It was screened from

the swamp by a gloomy line of weeping willows and evergreens. Once you swung around the trees the castle came into view, a heap of weathered granite knee-deep in weeds and nettles. We don't mine much granite around this part of Connecticut, and before you ask any questions maybe I should explain that Strowan Castle, granite and all, originally came from Scotland. You see, quite a number of the old settlers around central Connecticut were Scottish. One of them, a fellow by the name of Jonathan Ferguson, made a fortune in selling the special tobacco we grow in the Connecticut Valley. Old Jonathan never married and always dreamed of going back to Scotland. When he did, he bought himself Strowan Castle in the Highlands and settled back to enjoy life. The only trouble was he couldn't. He missed Connecticut too much. Still he loved his new castle. So old Jonathan figured there was just one thing left to do— to move the castle over to America. Which he did by having the castle torn down and crated over to Connecticut. Come to think of it, I don't suppose there's many people in our country who can claim to have a Scottish castle right in their own back yard, the way we have.

I had meant to cut around the empty old building and continue on my way home. As I said, it was the night before Halloween and I guess maybe I had to prove something to myself. After all I was twelve and who believes in haunted houses anyway? Or haunted castles for that matter. I pushed back a rusty iron gate and more or less followed my feet up the weed-choked path to a big wooden door between two stone pillars.

"You're nuts, Jasper Trimble," I muttered to myself as I placed my hand on the door and pressed inwards. It creaked open and I felt a wave of stale, damp air sweep against my face. I stopped. My heart was thumping a lot faster than it should. My skin felt kind of tight too, as though I was wearing a size too small for my bones.

I glowered. What was there to be afraid of? It had been fifty years since anyone had lived in Strowan Castle. The last owner had been a Louella Scruggs, an elderly spinster. Miss Louella, an eccentric old lady from all accounts, was still something of a legend around Litchville. She had lived all by herself in the draughty old castle, rarely seeing anyone and going to the village only when she had to.

Emboldened by the knowledge that Miss Louella and all the other former inhabitants of Strowan Castle were long since dead and decently buried, I inched a few steps past the door. The worn floorboards creaked under my feet and I found myself in a huge room with a stone fireplace in one corner. My eyes were getting used to the half-light now and they moved slowly around the empty, musty-smelling room. It was enormous, with heavy rafters. I supposed it had once been used as a kind of living room. The end of a chandelier blackened with age slithered down from the ceiling like a long dark snake all poised to pounce on something. It gave me a kind of spooky feeling and I looked hastily away. There really wasn't much to see. A couple of old tables leaned against the wall. An ancient bureau, two of its four drawers gone, stood below a cracked mirror on the far side of the room. The bare floor was littered with plaster that had peeled from the ceiling. Two of the rafters had split in the middle and now hung crazily down like thick brown arms. A broken armchair, spilling horsehair, was drawn up in front of the fireplace. I guess Miss Louella must have sat there in the old days looking into the flames.

There was nothing on the mantlepiece over the fire-place. The walls were also bare except for a few shreds of dark brown paper here and there. At least I thought there was nothing on the walls until my eye caught the little square of color just above and to the right of the fireplace. It was a calendar of some kind with a faded picture of a hunting scene. The paper was yellow and stiff and curled up at the bottom. There was a date but the printing was faded and in an odd kind of fine script. I had to peer closely to read it—1720.

I stared. 1720! Now that was odd! Miss Louella had died about fifty years ago. Everybody around Litchville knew that. So what on earth was she doing with a 1720 calendar on the wall?

I was still staring, puzzled, when I heard the voice. It seemed to come from just behind me. A voice with an up and down lilt to it. "Och, now, and I forgot to turn the calendar! 1720! My, how the time flies, does it no'?"

I spun around and gaped in amazement at the speaker. He was a man of maybe twenty-five or thirty. His face was lean with a queer sort of paleness to it. So lean and so pale that I felt—crazy as it sounds—that the half-light which spilled in from the broken shutter behind him didn't seem so much to lap around his head as through it. His eyes were black as midnight and his hair was long and fastened in a bunch behind his neck. But it wasn't the face or his hair I was looking at. It was his dress. He was wearing a kilt of a light-colored red and green tartan. A Scottish tam—later Malcolm told me it was called a Balmoral bonnet—was perched at an angle on his head. He had on some kind of velvet jacket with mother-of-pearl buttons, and a bunch of white lace stuck out from the top of it and under his chin. His hands were as fine and as pale as his face. One of them rested on the handle of a curved sword that hung in its scabbard from his waist. The other pressed against the side of the bare wall as he waited for me to speak.

I had to jerk my jaw muscles twice to unhinge the words. Even then they came out small and cramped. "Who are you?" I finally managed.

"Malcolm. Malcolm MacDhu."

I goggled at the apparition. I didn't quite know what to say. After all, if you're in an abandoned old castle and some character in a fancy kilt suddenly appears out of nowhere and announces he's Malcolm MacDhu, what would you say? Probably the same thing I said. "Oh, Malcolm MacDhu."

His proud head went back and his fingers tightened on that crazy sword of his. I must admit that by this time it was getting me more than just a little nervous. The next words out of his mouth didn't exactly help matters either.

"My father was Donald MacDhu, chief of the great Clan MacDhu of Gilnochie."

I wet my lips and started to edge nervously backwards. "Is that so?" I managed. Clearly I was face to face with some kind of nut. The sooner I got out of here the better.

He left the spot where he had been standing and strolled over to the fireplace. He didn't make any sound and I was puzzled for a moment for I remembered how the rotted boards had squeaked when I entered. I glanced down at the floor, littered with the chipped plaster from the ceiling. Only as I stared did understanding finally come. I felt my skin go cold. *There were no footprints on the plaster where he had walked!*

He must have noticed the look of horror on my face. He smiled. "Now, now, there's no need at all to be alarmed, lad. No need at all."

I said in a whisper, "What are you doing here?"
"I live here."
"But—but nobody lives in Strowan Castle."
"Except the ghost."
"The—" I stopped and he smiled gently.
"I'm the ghost."

CHAPTER TWO

I GUESS neither of us said anything for the next two minutes. I know for sure one of us didn't. Me. Even if I had felt like talking which somehow I didn't, what do you say to a ghost? I'll bet that even with practice it's not easy. And I don't have to tell you I didn't have any practice. I just stood where I was, my tongue as lifeless as my legs, my heart pounding like crazy.

It was the ghost who finally spoke first. "What's your name, lad?"

"Jasper. Jasper Trimble," I whispered. The words sounded strange in my ears, like the words of a stranger. Maybe they were. I stared again at the thin pale face of the figure in the kilt. Only then, as I peered more closely did I realize I had been right the first time. The light from the window behind the figure was seeping through his face! Not sharp or clear, but the soft glow was there just the same. I shrank back. "I can see through you!" I blurted out in horror.

He shrugged slightly. "It is my ectoplasm. That's what

I use when I want to materialize. I have to be careful how I use it or it runs down. Aye, and something else. My father, Donald MacDhu, chief of the Clan MacDhu of Gilnochie, was always a saving man himself, a cautious man with a shilling they said. Perhaps I take after him. Besides, we Scots are no' a people given to lavish spending." His dark eyes twinkled. "Anyway, what is so terrible, lad, about your being able to see through me? You will find many people in this life, I doubt not, as equally transparent as myself, and with less cause."

I nodded, not quite sure what he was getting at.

"So you will be called Jasper, eh?" he said. His voice seemed to go up and down gently when he spoke and I wondered if maybe it had anything to do with being a MacDhu. I mean anybody who goes around saving ectoplasm could just as well feel he ought to be saving breath too.

"That's right," I replied. "Jasper Trimble."

"And you live here?"

"Here?" I exclaimed, startled, looking around the huge room.

He waved an elegant arm. "Not here in Strowan Castle! No one has lived here since that silly old woman died; aye, and thank the good Lord for that! I thought He would never take her! Maybe He wasn't anxious to have her, knowing what an auld nuisance she was. Now what was her name—"

"Miss Louella. Miss Louella Scruggs."

"That was it!" Malcolm's face kind of darkened. "Always creeping around the castle in that nightgown of hers. Aye, and with a candle in her hand. Scared me half to life she did, the old busybody! Was certainly glad when she finally died."

"She scared you?" I asked. My voice seemed to be coming back. I suppose by this time I was getting used to the idea of speaking to a ghost.

Malcolm shook his head gloomily. "You had to see her, Jasper! Forever mumbling to herself and poking at the fire! Sometimes I think she suspected I was around. She would stop, a sly look to her face, and cast a quick look over her shoulder, as though to catch me off guard. No' that I ever let her see me, mind you. Still, she gave me a fair start more than once. Aye, I was glad enough when the Lord called her home, though I'm thinking He must have had to call her at the top of His lungs, for she was as deaf as a post."

Maybe it was the idea of a ghost being afraid of a harmless old spinster like Louella Scruggs that brought back some of my courage. I stopped my slow retreat towards the door. "You're a ghost?" I said. "But nobody believes in ghosts anymore."

"I do." He looked hurt. "It makes a difference when you *are* one."

I nodded. He had a point.

"Two hundred and fifty years! A long time to be a ghost."

"It's a long time to be anything," I said.

His face was thoughtful. "Two hundred and fifty years. A long time to be haunting the same house. It's been quite pleasant, though, in Strowan Castle. A wee bit draughty at times, and me with just this kilt besides."

I stared. Something was wrong. I said, "You've been haunting Strowan Castle for two hundred and fifty years?"

"That will be right, lad."

"There's only one thing, Mr. MacDhu—"

"Malcolm!" he interrupted impatiently. "You may call me Malcolm. I'm not that old!"

"There's only one thing, Malcolm. How could you have lived in Strowan Castle for two hundred and fifty years when they brought it over to America just before the Revolutionary War?"

He waved his hand airily. "Simply explained. When Jonathan Ferguson bought Strowan Castle he bought me too! And when he shipped the castle to America I came along with everything else in it! After all, where else was I to go, lad? Who wants a ghost around the house? Strowan Castle was my home, the only one I had ever known, man and ghost. Besides, there had always been a MacDhu in Strowan Castle. I couldn't bide the thought that our castle would be far off in America and no' a

MacDhu in it, at all, at all. So I stowed away in one of Mr. Ferguson's crates. I should mention that when I'm no' materialized I don't take up much space." He suddenly scowled. "Och, now and it was horrible for certain! Me, Malcolm MacDhu, son of the chief of all the MacDhus of Gilnochie, locked up in a crate! Aye, and seasick besides!"

I said, "I didn't know a ghost could get seasick."

"Did you ever ask one?" he grumbled. "Well, never mind. When we got to America Mr. Ferguson put the castle up just the way it had been in Scotland. I'll tell you here, Jasper, that all the way over I had been more than just a wee bit nervous about what I would find in America. I had heard all this talk about the savages in this country. Aye, and later on there was a night when a man went by on a horse crying, 'The British are coming! The British are coming!' at the top of his lungs." Malcolm shook his head. "I waited up for them until dawn but they never came. Still, it gave me a grand fright, all right, all that horrible yelling in the middle of the night."

"That must have been one of Paul Revere's men," I said.

Malcolm shrugged. "He did no' mention his name. I suppose the man was in something of a hurry or he would no' have been galloping and yelling the way he was."

I was about to tell Malcolm about the war between

the colonies and King George III but decided to keep my mouth shut. Maybe he was a royalist and might be upset to learn his side had lost. Some people are funny about these things. Ghosts too, I imagine.

"So you like America?" I asked.

"What I've seen of it. The only part of it I was no' liking at all was that old Scruggs woman."

I hesitated. For the last few minutes I had been aware that something was bothering me. A small uneasiness that just wouldn't go away. Finally I said, "Malcolm, if I ask you something—a question—you won't mind?"

He glided to the battered mirror over the bureau. For a long moment he studied himself in the fly-specked, dusty glass. He smoothed the white lace under his chin. "Ask any question you want, lad." He smiled into the mirror. It was plain to see that this Malcolm MacDhu had a pretty good opinion of himself.

"How did you become a ghost?"

His fingers froze. I could see him watching me in the mirror. He said in a quiet voice, "What did you say?"

"How did you become a ghost? I mean, Malcolm, isn't it true that most people who die don't ever become ghosts? Yet you're a ghost. I just wondered how—" I stopped for he had turned his head away from the mirror and was staring straight at me. There was a queer kind of look in his eyes and the words I was going to speak somehow shriveled up back in my throat.

15

"That is a secret," he said stiffly after a long silence. "A secret I have told to no one."

"Oh," I said. It wasn't a very bright remark, but I'll tell you I wasn't feeling too bright at the moment. Malcolm MacDhu had this funny look in his eye and his fingers seemed to be tightening around the handle of that crazy sword of his. I was beginning to wish I hadn't brought the subject up.

Finally he shrugged as though he had just come to some kind of decision. "Och, and perhaps it will no' be mattering greatly after all these years that someone should know my shameful story. But it will no' be easy in the telling at all, at all, for well you must know I am a man of pride, and the son of the great Donald MacDhu besides." He suddenly pulled his shoulders back and glared down at me. "There will no' be many that can claim their father is chief of the Clan MacDhu of Gilnochie!"

"Not many at all!" I agreed hastily, as I backed away from the fierce figure in the kilt. "Listen, Malcolm, it's no business of mine how you became a ghost. Just forget I even asked you."

"Forget?" He shook his head. "One can never forget the word that is spoken. No, Jasper Trimble, you will hear my story. But not now. Tomorrow. At eight. I must have time to go over in my mind the events of that awful day two hundred and fifty years ago."

I stirred uneasily. Tomorrow night was Halloween. If

a fellow had to go ghost-calling, Valentine's Day or Ground-hog Day made a lot more sense than Spook Day. I wet my lips. "Well, you see, Malcolm, it's this way. Tomorrow night is Halloween and—"

"That will be all," he interrupted. "Have I no' given you my word? The word of a MacDhu of Gilnochie? That word is no' given lightly. Tomorrow night, then. At eight. Until then—farewell!"

"But tomorrow's Halloween!" I cried. I guess it was more a wail than a cry. "I promised to go—" I stopped and stared, bug-eyed. Malcolm's buckled shoes were growing dim. All at once they were gone. They were followed a moment later by his bare knees and the sporran in front of his kilt. Now there was only half of Malcolm visible, the top half, and it seemed to be floating gently in space. I swallowed the rest of my words. There didn't seem to be much point in talking to only half of Malcolm. Besides, even *that* was slowly disappearing into thin air until only Malcolm's head remained visible. It drifted over to the open door at the far side of the room, then before I knew what had happened it too was gone. I was alone.

I stood quite still, my legs weak as water, my heart racing. The room was empty. In the broken mirror over the bureau I could see my frightened face. Then slowly, as the moments passed, my courage started to return. I looked around me. The chandelier still hung crazily from the ceiling. The chair with the broken springs still sat before the fireplace. Everything was as it had been before. Surely I must have imagined the whole crazy business! Or maybe I had been daydreaming. That was it. Miss Parkinson at school is forever telling me I daydream during language arts. That old calendar over there. Of course! That's what had started me off! I had been staring at it when—

I stopped, my eyes riveted on the door at the far side of the room. It was closing! Slowly. Soundlessly. And surely. The wind, of course. I wheeled around and stared at the faded drapes by the window. They hung motionless in the still air. Only the door moved. Only that. Then with a soft *click* it closed.

As fast as my trembling legs could carry me I bolted out of Strowan Castle.

CHAPTER THREE

I DON'T have to tell you that I didn't sleep too well that night. A lot of thoughts were crowding my mind when I crawled into bed. I kind of hoped they would be gone after I dozed off but they were all waiting for me when I woke up the next morning. And most of them were about a ghost named Malcolm MacDhu.

I keep a small stand-up calendar from the Wethersfield Branch of the Society for Saving on the chest of drawers next to my bed. The bank gives them to people who save there. The only thing I've been able to save so far is the stand-up calendar. That's because you need lots of money if you want to be a real saver. And if you have lots of money who needs a bank anyway, even a nice one that gives away calendars?

Well, as I was about to say before I interrupted myself, most mornings, unless it's Monday, I look at my calendar to see what day it is. Just in case, by some horrible accident I got things mixed up and showed up at school on a

Saturday. I'll bet you think nobody would ever do any-thing as nutty as that. But Rocky Bonelli did and Rocky's not nutty either. Rocky lives in a big farmhouse just across the way from us and hates school even more than I do. It was after what happened to Rocky that I got myself this nice little stand-up calendar from the bank. That was around the same time that Rocky Bonelli got his too, if I remember right.

Anyway, I didn't have to look at it this morning to know what day it was. I knew. Halloween. I groaned as I washed up. I had never felt so low.

Now maybe I should tell you here that I've always looked forward to Halloween. Only somehow I wasn't exactly looking forward to this one. Not with a two hundred and fifty year old spook named Malcolm Mac-Dhu waiting to give me the low-down on how he became a ghost. And in a deserted old castle yet. I scowled at myself in the mirror. *You're an idiot, Jasper Trimble! How could you ever have gotten yourself mixed up in such a crazy business? What were you trying to prove in the first place by going to Strowan Castle? No one would have*—I stopped, aware of a wave of vast relief deep within me. Of course! Why hadn't I thought about it before? No one had known that I had gone to Strowan Castle yesterday. No one would know—or care—if I didn't go tonight. No one, that is, except a certain Malcolm MacDhu. And why worry what an old ghost would think?

I brushed my teeth, rinsed my mouth and whistled the last of the toothpaste from between my teeth. I felt as though a mighty weight had just been lifted from my shoulders. With the knowledge that there was no reason on earth why I should have to go to the old castle, Halloween suddenly seemed its old self again. Let's see now. First of all, I'd go over to Rocky's after supper and talk things over with him. Rocky always had a lot of great ideas. Especially on Halloween.

I hadn't said anything to Mom and Pop about what had happened yesterday. To begin with, I didn't think they would have believed me. They've got this weird idea that I'm some kind of a jokester and Mom would most likely have smiled patiently and said, "Is that so, Jasper? A two hundred and fifty year old ghost named Malcolm MacDhu? Well, well. Now finish your cereal and put your bowl in the sink when you're done." As for telling my sister Debbie, that was out too. Debbie's eight years older than me and likes to show how superior she is. Her nose kind of wrinkles when she sees me coming, especially when she's got her boyfriend, Albert Hooplewaite, over at the house. Not that we don't normally get along pretty well together. I'm talking about Debbie and me, not Albert. What a creep *he* is. I'll tell you about Albert later. Anyway, to get back to what I was saying, I had made up my mind that it just wouldn't have made sense to tell anyone about the ghost in Strowan Castle. Now that I had decided not to keep my appointment with Malcolm MacDhu I was more than ever glad that for once I had kept my mouth shut.

It was queer, though, how as the day wore on I somehow felt less and less pleased with myself. I couldn't figure out for the life of me just what was bugging me. I guessed it had something to do with Strowan Castle for every time I happened to think of the old mansion I got this same squirmy feeling. Almost as though I had done something wrong, something I was ashamed of. Yet what had I to be ashamed of? I asked myself. Just because I wasn't going to keep that crazy date with Malcolm Mac-Dhu? Why should I? I had other things to do with my time on Halloween than listen to a ghost story. Especially when the one telling the story happened to be the ghost.

Pop was upstairs working on one of his paintings when I got back from school. The main reason we bought the old Moore farmhouse five years ago was because Pop wanted a quiet place where he could get away from everybody and paint. The sprawling old house needed lots of repair but it had many rooms including two tucked away by themselves on the third floor. They were tiny with a small window in each and I guess you might say they were attics. Pop took over the larger one and called it his *atelier*. That's a fancy French word for a work shop but sounds a lot better. When Pop isn't teaching at the Litchville Community College he's painting in his atelier. He's a better teacher than he's a painter, I guess, because he never has been able to sell anything. That doesn't seem to bother him too much. He says Vincent van Gogh never sold anything either, except maybe to his brother, and that didn't count.

"What are you painting, Pop?" I asked as I tossed my books on a chair and stared at the squiggly lines on the easel. I should tell you that Pop is going through something he calls his Abstract Period. That means he paints things different from what they look like. I do too but Pop says he does it intentionally. I suppose that makes a difference.

He stepped back from the easel and stared kind of moodily at it. He scowled. "It's not coming along the way it should, Jasper. The same old trouble."

"What trouble?" I asked.

He shook his head. "I wish I knew. If it was someone else's picture I'd know. I just *feel* somehow that it's all wrong."

"Looks all right to me," I said, screwing one eye shut and peering out of the other. I found out a while ago that I can see better that way. Especially when I'm looking at abstract paintings and things like that.

"You like it?" he asked. For some reason he seemed even gloomier than before.

I nodded. "Super."

He sighed. "Must be even worse than I thought it was," he said in a funny, sad sort of voice.

I squinted again at the maze of lines and colored shapes on the canvas. "What's it supposed to be, Pop?" I asked helpfully. "If I knew what you're driving at maybe I could at least tell you if you're getting warm."

He got kind of red looking and I wondered if perhaps some of his paint had got smeared on his face.

"If I get any warmer, Jasper Trimble, I'll—I'll explode! You and your everlasting questions!" He threw his palette knife on the floor and for a moment I was afraid he was going to have some kind of fit. Finally he calmed down, then he grinned a little. He draped his arm around my shoulder. "Sorry, Jasper. It's not your fault. It's mine. Thinking I can do abstracts! Maybe I should go back to what I feel I do best, painting apples and red Connecticut barns and things like that."

I said quickly, "Sure, Pop," for I don't like to see him upset, and he can get awfully upset over his painting sometimes. Pop says you've got to feel strongly about what you're painting, although it beats me how anybody can get worked up over creepy stuff like apples and red Connecticut barns. I guess that's why most painters are different from normal people.

We were just finishing supper later on when Mom glanced at the clock over the stove. "Seven thirty. Aren't you going out trick-or-treating tonight, Jasper? It's Halloween, you know."

I shook my head. "Kid stuff. Strictly for juniors! Think

I'll just stay home and curl up with a good spook. Ha ha!"

Debbie made a face at me. "Must you, Jasper? You and your frightful jokes."

"How about your frightful jokes?" I replied. Debbie can be okay but she can get me awfully mad when she starts putting on her Big Sister act. Like now.

Her eyebrows went up. "My frightful jokes?"

"Like Albert Hooplewaite, that boyfriend of yours. The one with the beard—"

"You shut up, Jasper," she fairly hissed at me. "Albert wears that beard for a purpose—"

"Yeah, he hates barbers," I cut in. I was beginning to feel like my old self again. Just then Pop lowered his paper and frowned across the table at me. I know Pop can't stand Albert Hooplewaite either, but he doesn't like me to talk about him. I was waiting for him to snap at me when he turned his head and looked over at Mom.

"That's funny," he mused, as though talking to himself.

Mom was rinsing the dishes before putting them into the washer. She turned off the water. "What's funny, Henry?"

"Why should anyone want to put up a high rise apartment around here? Especially when they will have to tear down the old Strowan Castle property to do it?"

I stared. "Strowan Castle?"

A Ghost Around the House

Pop nodded and glanced down at the copy of the Wethersfield *Post* he had been reading. "Here's what it says in the article. '*The Litchville Town Planning and Zoning Commission has recommended to the Town Council that approval be granted a zoning request for a proposed high density apartment. Specifically the commission recommended that the request by the Acme Realty Corporation for change of zone from RM-3 to RM-1 for eight adjacent land parcels, including the property known as Strowan Castle, be approved. It is expected that following the zone change and the Town Council consent, Acme Realty Corporation will proceed at once with the razing of the old castle which has long occupied the northeast corner of the property.*'"

"Strowan Castle?" I exclaimed in horror. "They're going to pull down Strowan Castle? But they can't do that! What would become of Malcolm?"

Mom looked at me curiously. "Malcolm? Who's Malcolm?"

"Oh don't mind him, Mother," Debbie cut in. "You know Jasper. He's in another world. I'll be quite happy to see that old pile torn down. It's just a fire trap and an eyesore."

"I'm still surprised, though," Pop said slowly. "After all, the old castle was part of Litchville, part of our history."

Debbie shrugged. "History, mystery! Who cares,

Daddy? Albert was saying just the other day that history has to be relevant to what's happening to mean anything."

Pop scratched his head. "Seems to me, Debbie, that the history I'm talking about just *has* to be relevant. For example, it was right next door in Wethersfield, in the old Joseph Webb house on Main Street, that George Washington and Count de Rochambeau met to complete their plans for the battle of Yorktown that signaled the end of the Revolutionary War. What happened then just had to have a relevancy to what's happening today." He paused. "Anyway, forgetting Strowan Castle for the moment, I must confess I'm surprised that anyone would want to put up a high density apartment over there by Dead Man's Swamp."

Mom dried her hands. "Dead Man's Swamp! That's a name to scare the daylights out of any real estate operator. I'll bet they get the council to rename it Litchville Everglades or something like that."

Pop nodded absently. "Strowan Castle. It's going to seem strange with that old pile of rocks gone. I can remember it as a boy—" He stopped and looked at me. "Where are you going, Jasper?"

"Out," I replied. I could feel my legs trembling. "I—I just remembered something—"

"Like tonight's Halloween," Debbie interrupted. "When the local ghosts go for their annual stroll." She laughed.

"Yeah," I said. I couldn't figure out what was so funny.

Pop frowned. "But I thought you said only a few minutes ago that it was kid stuff?" He eyed me curiously then shrugged and reached for his pipe. "Okay, Jasper, but don't be late. Halloween or no Halloween you have school tomorrow, remember that."

I said, "I'll remember, Pop." As I closed the door behind me I glanced over at the clock. Seven forty-five.

I had exactly fifteen minutes to get to Dead Man's Swamp, and my eight o'clock meeting with Malcolm MacDhu, the ghost of Strowan Castle.

CHAPTER FOUR

THE HUGE living room of Strowan Castle stood in darkness except for a narrow band of moonlight from an opening in one of the drapes. A musty odor seemed to fill my nose, like the smell you get in a damp cave or an old cellar. I waited by the door, my heart thumping against my ribs.

"Malcolm?" I whispered. "Are you there, Malcolm?" My lips felt like sandpaper against my tongue. Cautiously I inched one foot after the other until I reached what I felt must be the center of the room.

"Of course I'm here!" snapped a familiar voice from somewhere in the darkness just ahead of me. I almost leaped out of my skin.

"Where—" My eyes strained into the black void. "But —but I can't see you, Malcolm."

"Och, and it's daft I'm getting for certain! I'll no' be getting too many visitors. Just a minute, lad, while I turn on the ectoplasm."

"Take your time, Malcolm," I urged. All of a sudden I found I wasn't too eager to have an old ghost come floating out of the darkness towards me.

For a long moment there was nothing, then gradually a faint sort of glow started to creep into the blackness just ahead of me. It was greenish-white in color, if you could say it had a color, and at first it didn't seem to have any shape. It hung in the air, like some weird sort of luminous fog. I tell you, if my legs could have moved at that moment they would have moved me right out of Strowan Castle. Fast! The trouble was they seemed to have taken root on the floor and all I could do was do what I was already doing. Nothing. Including breathing. I guess, looking back, I had never been so scared at any time in my life as I was at that moment. Then all at once the phosphorescent mass started to weave itself into a form. A face came into view, a strong proud face with piercing eyes. The face was followed a few seconds later by a pair of shoulders, then by a kilt, a sword, tartan stockings and finally by a pair of silver-buckled shoes. It was Malcolm MacDhu all right, if not in the flesh at least in spirit.

"So you came," he said. "Good. I was a wee bit afraid you might no' come back, it being Halloween. I can see now that you are a lad of courage. Aye, like myself once if the truth be told."

"Look Malcolm," I began, "I have some news for you."

"Good news?"

He must have seen me shake my head in the darkness for he waved his hand impatiently in the air. "If it is no' good news then it is bad and the devil with it say I. Besides, bad news like strong cheese never spoils by keeping. We will get to it later."

"But this is important! I would never have come here except I had to tell you!"

"Later." Again he waved one of his hands. "Yesterday I'm minding you asked me a question. A question I said I would answer. Did I no' give you my word? Let us hear no more about it. There is a chair just a wee bit over to your left. Sit."

"But—"

"Sit!" he thundered.

I groped hastily in the darkness, found the chair and sank down into it. Maybe Malcolm was right at that. Maybe bad news could keep. Like strong cheese.

"My story, Jasper, is one of pride. Pride of self. I tell it to you for one reason, that you may avoid the fate that has been mine since old Calum Carnoustie laid his curse on me that evil day, October 31, 1720. The curse has denied me the peace of the grave and bids me walk the world eternally as the spirit you now see me.

"First of all, you will be understanding that the Mac-Dhus were a proud clan, aye, and none prouder. And of all the proud MacDhus none was prouder than myself, for was I no' the son of the mighty Donald MacDhu himself, the chief of all the MacDhus of Gilnochie?

"No one needs to be ashamed, lad, to be proud. If a man sets a good value on his worth and the worth is there, that will no' be a bad thing, at all, at all. But when pride becomes vanity and the man becomes blind to his own flaws, then it is an evil thing." There was a long, painful pause. "I was a vain man. Vain of many things. My cunning as a hunter. My valor as a soldier. My talent as a painter. But of nothing was I more proud than my skill as a horseman.

"Och, and it was the bonnie rider I was myself, if I must say so! The fancy of all the lassies and the envy of all the lads as I swept low in the saddle across the heather after the panting fox! No, none more swift in the chase than Malcolm MacDhu. No, nor none with a grander conceit of himself than the same one.

"It was on this October morning that it happened, Jasper. I had taken my horse to the smithy for a new shoe. The smithy lent me his own horse, Jenny, for I had to ride over to the village of Dunstane on some business.

"You will understand, lad, that this Jenny was no ordinary horse at all. Och, now, and far from it! Jenny was the oldest, sleepiest, most gentle horse in all of the country around Gilnochie. She could no' move at all beyond a trot, and that down a brae with a wind at her back.

"Now I must tell you that I was just a wee bit embarrassed as I rode that morning over to Dunstane. After all, was I no' Malcolm MacDhu, the finest horseman in all Gilnochie, and the son of the chief of the great Clan MacDhu besides? So, like a coward, I took the back roads to Dunstane fearful that someone might see me and laugh. I was never a man to be laughed at, then or now.

"Jenny was plodding along through the heather when all at once it happened. Lost in thought I never saw the branch of the big tree above me. At the last moment I looked and felt something crash against my poor skull. So hard was the blow that I was flung clear over old Jenny's head. I never remembered hitting the ground, never remembered anything, lad, until I recovered consciousness hours later right here in this very room."

I jumped. "Here?" I exclaimed.

"Aye, here. Did I no' tell you that Strowan Castle was the ancestral home of the chief of the MacDhus? It was right on the spot where you are sitting that I came to. There were about forty people gathered around me. All of them were that solemn faced too, and nobody said anything. My father's eyes were red and I knew fine he had been weeping. Calum Carnoustie was there also. Calum was the oldest man in Gilnochie. There were many that said old Calum had the gift of the second sight and was in league with the kelpies who lived in the pool at the foot of the glen. Everyone was staring at me gloomily and I realized in my heart I must be dying.

"Nobody spoke at all but I knew the question on everyone's lips. How could it have happened that Malcolm MacDhu, the finest horseman in all Gilnochie, should fall from a horse such as Jenny? I could feel my strength fading and I was on the point of telling them what had actually happened when something held me back. How could I leave this world and have people remember—with many a chuckle—that Malcolm Mac-Dhu had tumbled from an old horse and broken his head? Dying as I was, I could feel the fierce shame of it. Och, and it wasn't to be borne at all, at all! I spoke the first words that came to my lips.

" 'It was one of the traitorous MacMurchies who did it,' I whispered. 'He was watching me from a tree. As I passed under the spot where the same one was, he, blackhearted villian that he was, leaned down and struck me with his broadsword. I only caught a glimpse of the rogue before I fell. But there was no mistaking the dark green of the plaid around him. He was a MacMurchie.'

"I could hear the murmurs of shock and wrath all around me. My father leaped to his feet, his eyes blazing, the dagger he had pulled from his stocking stabbing the air. 'They shall pay for it!' he exclaimed as he brandished the wicked knife. 'Aye, and bitterly shall the men of the Clan MacMurchie rue the day they struck down in innocent blood the son of the chief of the MacDhus of Gilnochie!'

"Everyone was on his feet now, reaching for swords and battle-axes and hurling curses at the hated Mac-Murchies, our old enemies. Suddenly the angry voices died away as Calum Carnoustie got to his feet. He limped slowly over to where I lay dying and looked down at me.

" 'You lie, Malcolm MacDhu,' he cried. 'It is given me to know things that are no' revealed to other men. It was no MacMurchie who struck you down! It was your own pride and vanity! And it is that same pride and vanity that would cause us now to stain the heather with the blood of innocent men!' He stopped and thrust out a long bony finger at me. His eyes were blazing like two hot coals. 'You are cursed, Malcolm MacDhu,' he screamed, 'cursed to walk this earth as a spirit until such time as you atone for this deed. Cursed Malcolm Mac-Dhu. Cursed! Cursed! Cursed!' And with the curse of Calum Carnoustie ringing in my ears, I died in my father's arms.

"So now you know my story, Jasper Trimble. It is a sad story, is it no', for it has no ending at all. For how am I to atone for the lie that lay upon my lips as I died? So here I stay in Strowan Castle, until such time that the curse of old Calum Carnoustie is lifted and my spirit is allowed to rest in the quiet little kirkyard where my father sleeps with the MacDhus of Gilnochie."

I said nothing. What was there to say? Fear had long since left me. Now there was only a feeling of pity for the unhappy ghost of Strowan Castle. Yes, and a queer feeling of admiration, for I guessed it had not been easy for poor Malcolm to tell his story.

"You said you had news, Jasper. Something to tell me?"

"Oh?" So interested had I been in Malcolm's story that I had forgotten all about the reason that had brought me to the castle. Only now that I had heard the story was I suddenly aware it was going to be a lot harder to tell mine. I wet my lips. "Some other time, Malcolm," I blurted out hastily as I got to my feet.

He must have mistaken the reason why I was in a hurry to leave. He smiled. "No need at all to be afraid, lad. As long as you are in Strowan Castle, you are the guest of the MacDhus." His eyes traveled around the room. "Strowan Castle," he murmured, as though to himself. "It's been a long time."

If ever I was going to tell him it would have to be now. Besides, he was going to find out anyway. I took a deep breath. "They're going to tear it down, Malcolm!"

He frowned. "Tear what down, lad?"

"Strowan Castle."

He smiled. "It is a wee joke, eh, Jasper? Perhaps because it is Halloween? No one could tear Strowan Castle down. Not even our old enemies, the Clan MacMurchie."

I said, "Malcolm, it's not the Clan MacMurchie. It's

a company that's going to put up a high rise apartment.
It's in the newspapers too."

"But—but, I'm no' understanding at all." Malcolm's
voice was a wail of distress. "They *can't* do that! If they
put up this—this high rise thing there would be no more
Strowan Castle!"

I nodded. I had never felt so miserable.

"And if there's no more Strowan Castle—" His voice
died away and he didn't finish whatever he was going to
say.

"I'm sorry, Malcolm," I said. "I told you it was bad
news."

I don't know if he heard me. "No more Strowan Castle," he whispered. "Och, and it's no' to be believed at
all. And me? What's to become of me? Who ever heard
of a ghost haunting a high rise apartment?" He laughed
bitterly.

I don't know where the words came from but they
were on my lips and I spoke them. "You can move in
with us."

He stared. "With you?"

"We've got an old farmhouse just a short ways from
here. Of course it's not a castle but we've got lots of space
and nobody would bother you. Maybe only Albert
Hooplewaite, who's Debbie's boyfriend and wears a
beard, but you don't have to listen to him. As a matter of
fact, you don't even have to see him. There's an empty

room next to Pop's atelier you can have. Nobody will even know you're around."

Malcolm said nothing for ten, maybe twenty seconds. Finally, he eyed me suspiciously. "You are sure you are no' doing this, lad, because you're sorry for me? If there is one thing I can no' bide it is people feeling sorry for me. Me, Malcolm MacDhu, the son of the chief—" He swallowed hard, then said in a small voice, "No fuss, Jasper. I hate fuss."

"No fuss, Malcolm," I promised. "And don't worry. Everything will work out. Pop will be busy with his painting, and oh—you've just got to come! You've just got to! And there's something else. I think it's gonna be fun!"

He regarded me gloomily. "What's going to be fun?"

I grinned. "Having a ghost around the house!"

CHAPTER FIVE

I DIDN'T tell anyone about Malcolm, of course, not even Rocky Bonelli. After all, who was going to believe me? Besides, it could hardly do Malcolm any good if word got around that the Trimbles were going to have a two hundred and fifty year old non-paying boarder staying with them. Come to think of it, it would hardly do the Trimbles any good either.

I couldn't get Malcolm to think of leaving his old home until they started to bring up the bulldozers and the heavy trucks. He stared with shock and horror in his eyes the day a huge iron ball crashed against one of the castle walls and sent the masonry flying.

"Why—why?" was all he could say and I mumbled something Albert had mentioned once about Progress. Malcolm didn't answer. Maybe he hadn't heard me. Or maybe, coming from the eighteenth century he didn't know what the word meant. It's not an easy word to explain sometimes. Not even in the twentieth century.

A Ghost Around the House

With the destruction of Strowan Castle underway, Malcolm finally agreed it was time to get out. I guess it would have hurt him very much to have seen his old home torn apart right before his eyes. I'll bet not many people can say they have lived in the same house for over two hundred years.

Malcolm moved into our place that night. We both felt it would make things a lot easier if he remained invisible while I sneaked him over to the house. I don't have to tell you that you don't see too many guys in kilts strolling around Litchville. Or Wethersfield for that matter.

The worst part was getting Malcolm into the house but it went off a lot better than I had expected. Actually as Malcolm was invisible there really wasn't anything to worry about. The only bad moment was when I held the door open for Malcolm and Mom asked me why I was letting all that cold air into the house. As I couldn't see him, it was hard to tell whether he was in or out, so I had to go real slow in closing the door while Mom kept getting madder and madder about all the cold air. Anyway, everything worked out fine and I finally got him up to the small room next to Pop's atelier. I turned on the light. "Okay, Malcolm, we're here. It's not exactly a castle but it's home."

It took him a few moments before he materialized. He was sitting on a small rocking chair by the window.

He nodded to himself as his eyes took in the room. I could see he wasn't too unhappy. It took a load off my mind for frankly I had been kind of worried he would find the Trimble farm an awful letdown from Strowan Castle. Finally he got up from the chair, smoothed the sporran on his kilt and strutted over to the mirror above the desk. He seemed his old conceited self again as he looked at himself in the glass. "That bonnie lassie downstairs, with the blond hair and the blue eyes, who would she be now?"

"What?" I exclaimed. "What bonnie lassie?" I stared at him, shocked. "You can't mean my sister Debbie? She's the one I told you about. The one who goes with that creep Albert."

"So that will be Debbie," Malcolm murmured. He touched the bunch of lace under his chin. "I like her."

"You do?"

Malcolm nodded and adjusted the pin on a large, yellow stone that held the plaid around his shoulder. "Och, now, and if I was only a couple of hundred years younger," he exclaimed with a soft sigh of regret.

I grunted. "Debbie's okay. I mean now and then. Mostly, though, she's as kooky as Albert. They were sitting on the couch when we came in. Albert was the one with the beard."

"And your father, Jasper, I'm minding you said he's a painter?"

41

I nodded. "You'll see a lot of Pop. After he finishes at school he works in the room next to yours. He tries awfully hard and he knows an awful lot about art and things like that. It's just that somehow none of his paintings ever *click*."

"I see," Malcolm said with a purr. He rubbed his hands together. "Well, well." He coughed and looked at me slyly. "I—er—may have mentioned to you, lad, that I was quite the painter myself in the old days; aye, quite the painter indeed." He flicked a thread from his black velvet jacket. "Perhaps I will be able to give your father a wee bit of help now and then."

I frowned. "You'd better be careful. Pop can be awfully funny about some things."

Malcolm smiled airily. "Aye, but he would like to be famous, would he no'?"

"Yes, but—"

"But nothing, Jasper," he protested. "It is the least I can do to show my gratitude!"

I looked at him uneasily. There was something in Malcolm's innocent eyes that I wasn't sure I liked. Still, if he could help Pop become famous, what could be wrong with that? I shrugged the misgivings from my mind and crossed over to the door. "I'd better be getting downstairs or they'll be wondering where I am. See you later."

Mom had put away the last of the supper dishes and

Pop was reading when I got back to the living room. He put down the paper and glanced over at Mom. "Now that's odd."

"What's odd, Henry?" Mom asked.

"This item here in the Wethersfield *Post*. It claims that the wreckers found a calendar with a 1720 date on it hanging on the walls of Strowan Castle. Now what on earth would a 1720 calendar be doing there?"

Debbie put down the picture album she had been showing Albert and frowned. "It is strange, Daddy. I mean that would be before they brought Strowan Castle over from Scotland. Do you suppose it could have belonged to Louella Scruggs? I've often heard she collected antiques for the old dump."

"It's not a dump, Debbie," I said hotly, "it's a castle."

"Was, Jasper," Albert Hooplewaite corrected me. Albert is always correcting people. He wears glasses but looks over the top of them when he speaks to you. I figured out that the only time he looks through them is when he's looking at his beard. It's a pretty scraggly mess from the front but maybe it comes out a lot different when you're seeing it from the back. I hope so.

"Castles, Jasper," he said, in the voice he uses when he's explaining things, "are relics of a feudalistic society that has no relevance to the issues and values of today." In case you're wondering, maybe I should mention that Albert Hooplewaite uses words like that all the time.

"I like castles," I said for no particular reason other than to disagree with Albert.

He tossed me a pitying look from somewhere behind the thatch on his face. "No one likes castles," he corrected again. "Some people *think* they do but it is merely a romantic nostalgia that has been planted and fostered by certain elements of our corrupt middle class society to suit its own corrupt middle class purposes."

"Ghosts like castles," I retorted. It wasn't an awfully bright remark but it was the best I could come up with at the moment. Anyway, I was getting pretty fed up with Albert's highfalutin talk. I don't know exactly what middle class is but at least it sounds a lot better than second class.

Albert stared at me, then turned to Debbie. "Don't tell me the boy believes in ghosts?"

I said nettled, "Well, some people do."

"I am afraid, Jasper, that some people are—well, let's be charitable and say they are gullible." Albert smiled, or I think he did, for his beard twitched. "You must understand that the ghost fixation is nothing more or less than a sinister device conceived by the Establishment for the enslavement of the lower classes. It is a romantic smoke screen behind which they hide—" He suddenly leaped up from the couch, grasping the back of his neck.

Debbie stared at him. "Albert! What's the matter?"

Albert's face was white. Or the top of it was and I guess the rest was too. "Something touched me just now!"

"Touched you?" Debbie's eyes were wide in her head. She looked around. "But there's no one here, Albert. You must have imagined it."

He nodded uncertainly. "Maybe it was all that talk about ghosts. A psychosomatic reaction triggered by my total absorption in what I was discussing at the moment." He frowned and his fingers returned to his neck. "Queer, though, it felt so real. Like an ice-cold hand."

Mom glanced over from the portable typewriter she was using to type up the minutes of the Litchville Garden Club. "A draft most likely. Maybe somebody left the upstairs door open. Sometimes when the wind blows a certain way we get these cold air currents."

I looked warily around the room. It had to be Malcolm. I remembered clearly closing the door upstairs before coming downstairs. He must have followed me and no doubt had heard Albert's speech and thought he would have a little fun. Maybe he was still around. I groaned. I hoped he wouldn't do anything crazy. At least not on his first night in our house.

"What's the matter with your cat?" Albert said sharply.

I glanced over at Cleo. Now normally our calico cat sleeps eighteen hours a day. The rest of the time she lolls around yawning and waiting for the eighteen hours to happen. I mean she's *lazy*. Only she didn't look lazy now. Her back was arched and her hair was bristling and she was staring straight ahead as though she had just seen a ghost. Maybe she had.

"Must be a mouse," Debbie said. "Funny, though, we haven't had any around here since we got Cleo."

"A mouse?" Albert exclaimed. "Just look at her. She's scared stiff! She looks as though she has just seen a saber-toothed tiger." He scowled over his glasses. "What kind of mice do you have around here anyway?" He grunted as Cleo slowly relaxed. "She seems to be all right now."

Mom looked up from her typewriter. "Cats are funny."

Albert wet his lips. "Yeah," he said. "I suppose."

I got up. With Cleo her old self again I figured that Malcolm had left the room and was back upstairs. The little incident with Cleo had scared me though. The others might get suspicious. I hoped the cat wouldn't have too much trouble getting used to the idea of having a ghost around the house.

Malcolm was waiting for me in the room upstairs when I got there. He was grinning and I could see he was mighty pleased with himself as he sat in his rocking chair by the window.

"So Albert will no' be believing in the likes of ghosts,

will he now? Well, well! Still, I would no' have believed in the likes of Albert if I had no' met the same one." He rocked soundlessly in his chair and then chuckled. "Did you see the man jump when I touched him?"

I frowned. "You shouldn't have done that, Malcolm."

He looked hurt. "Och, now Jasper, I have to have some fun now and then. I must tell you I was always a very—what is the word now?—*spirited* lad." His dark eyes twinkled mischievously.

"Joke," I said bitterly. "Look, Malcolm, if they find out you're here we could be in trouble."

"Nonsense," returned Malcolm in that airy way of his. He produced a silver snuffbox from the leather sporran on his kilt. His nostrils twitched as he inhaled. "You heard Albert. He will be like all the others. They will no' believe in ghosts. What was it now he said I was? '*A sinister device conceived by the Establishment for the enslavement of the lower classes.*'" He laughed and shook his powdered head. "I have been called many things back in Gilnochie but never that! So do no' be alarmed, lad. No matter if you told them there was a ghost in the house they would no' be believing you."

"No?" I asked doubtfully.

"No." He glanced down at his legs. They were beginning to disappear. "The ectoplasm. It's been acting queer since I left Strowan Castle. Maybe it would be best if I just shut it off now altogether. I don't like it at all, at all when I'm no' seeing my feet. I miss them. Fine you know, Jasper, I have always been greatly attached to them." There was a tiny chuckle from somewhere just ahead of me only it was hard to say from exactly where because Malcolm MacDhu of Gilnochie had vanished.

But if he had vanished he had not gone. For all at once the empty rocking chair by the window started to sway backwards and forwards. I felt the hair on the back of my neck start to rise. There was something real creepy about the empty chair rocking all by itself.

"See you tomorrow, Malcolm," I cried as I bolted from the room. "Got some homework to do."

I almost fell over Cleo in my haste to get down the stairs.

CHAPTER SIX

Rocky Bonelli walked home from school with me the next day. I had whispered to him hurriedly when Miss Wagner left the language arts room for a moment that I had something to tell him later. Now we were sitting on the old weatherbeaten sulky that graced the front yard of the Bonelli house, our legs dangling over the side.

Rocky glanced at me curiously. "Okay, Jasper, out with it. What's the big secret?"

"Huh?"

"Look, I can read you like a book." He grunted. "Better, considering how I read *some* books. Anyway, it's as plain as the ears on an elephant you've got something you want to spill. Okay, spill it." He rolled a stick of gum up into a ball and popped it into his mouth.

I took a deep breath. "We've got a ghost in the house."

He sputtered and I thought for a moment the chewing gum had got stuck in his windpipe. "You've got a what?" he exclaimed finally.

"A ghost." I thought maybe I'd better explain further. "His name's Malcolm MacDhu."

"Oh, sure, *that's* his name." Rocky's eyes seemed kind of large for his head and he started to edge down the sulky away from me.

"Look, Rocky, I'm not crazy if that's what you're thinking. As a matter of fact, Malcolm warned me only last night that nobody would believe me. I thought I'd tell you just the same. I mean when you've got a ghost around the house, you've got to tell somebody."

Rocky nodded. "Yeah. I mean you can't wait around for somebody to ask you." He had stopped edging down the old wagon. He stared at me suspiciously out of his right eye. "How come you never saw him before?"

I shrugged. "He just moved in."

"He just moved in?"

"Last night."

"But—but—Jasper—just like that?"

"Well, no, Rocky. You see I asked him to come over—"

Rocky's jaws, which had been methodically chomping at his wad of gum, suddenly froze. His mouth remained open. Solemnly he fished out a paper wrapper from his pocket. Solemnly he popped the gum into the paper. He turned his head. "Say that again?"

"Look, Rocky. If I say everything again and you keep repeating what I say, I'll never get done. Now if you'll just keep still for a couple of minutes, I'll tell you everything that's happened. Right from the beginning."

"That's a good place to begin," Rocky said.

He didn't say any more until I had filled him in on everything that had happened. I could see when I was finished that he was impressed. I could also see he still wasn't too convinced.

"But a ghost, Jasper!" he exclaimed. "Nobody believes in ghosts anymore. If you told one of the teachers in school you had just been shooting the breeze with a two hundred and fifty year old ghost named Malcolm Mac-Dhu, do you know what she would do? Quick like a bunny she'd have some guy in a white coat checking the bumps on your head."

"Yeah," I admitted gloomily.

"Yeah, again," Rocky said. He scowled over at our farm across the way and I could see he wanted to believe me but didn't know how. "When did you first see him?"

"The night before Halloween."

Rocky's eyes lit up triumphantly. "See what I mean? Halloween! You were thinking about ghosts and all that spooky jazz and just imagined it all."

I shook my head. Malcolm had been right after all. Rocky Bonelli was my best friend. If Rocky couldn't believe me, who could? "Honestly, Rocky, I didn't imagine it. How do you go about making up a guy with a handle like Malcolm MacDhu? And he's not a ghost like you'd think a ghost would be. I mean he doesn't go around in a long white sheet, wailing. He gets mad easy, and he's funny and he's sad and I never met anyone so proud of himself—" I stopped. "You don't make up people like that, Rocky. You just don't."

"Hm. Look. I'm not saying there isn't a ghost in your house, but I'm not saying there is one either, okay?" He gave me a slightly worried look as he hopped down from the sulky. "I wouldn't say too much about this to anyone. You know how people are. See you later."

"See you," I said.

A lot of thoughts were spinning around in my head as I watched Rocky retreat up the path to his house. Clearly nobody was going to have much faith in any story I told about an old ghost. For a reason I could not have explained, even to myself, the knowledge that nobody would know, or care, what happened to Malcolm filled me with a queer sort of sadness. How would Malcolm ever hope to end the curse that old Calum Carnoustie had brought down on him? He needed help, but how could anyone help him when they didn't believe he even existed? Poor Malcolm! If things had been tough for him before, it looked as though they might be a lot tougher from here on in.

"Something will be wrong, lad?" Malcolm darted a quick glance at me, then resumed his rocking.

"Huh?" I exclaimed, confused. "Nothing, Malcolm.

Nothing at all." I looked away hastily for I did not want him to see my face.

His eyebrows went up. "Nothing at all? Och, Jasper, and it's plain enough to see that something is bothering you." He gazed out of the window at the Bonelli farm across the way. "That lad who was with you now. Who was he?"

"Rocky. Rocky Bonelli."

"He's your friend?"

I nodded.

He was silent for a long moment. "I see," he said quietly. "And you told him about me, eh? And he does no' believe you."

I stared. "How did you know?"

He shrugged good-naturedly. "It's simple enough. One does no' live as long as I have without learning something of human nature. I told you last night that no one would believe you if you told them you had a ghost around the house. But you had to tell someone anyway. I watched you just a few moments ago with your friend. I saw him staring off curiously at this house. I followed him with my eyes as he left and you frowned after him. Then you made your way home, looking glum and upset. So I put two and two together. As I was saying, it was simple enough." He paused and stopped the motion of the chair. "And I was right," he said softly. "He did no' believe you."

"No," I said, "he did not believe me."

He got up from his chair. "Well, let us no' talk any more about it. By the way, I was looking at that painting your father will be working on. It's no' so bad. No' so bad at all."

"You think so?" I asked doubtfully. "I mean Pop tries hard and he knows an awful lot about art. It's just that he doesn't seem to get anywhere."

Malcolm strutted over to the mirror and studied himself. I never saw anyone who spent so much time looking at himself. I guess if you don't have too many people around to look at, you wind up looking at yourself. It was just that Malcolm seemed to *enjoy* it. Maybe being the son of the chief of all the MacDhus of Gilnochie does something to you.

"I may have mentioned, Jasper, that I was quite the clever painter myself once." He smiled with satisfaction at his reflection in the glass. "Quite the clever painter indeed. Aye, I might have gone far with my talent if I had lived a wee bit longer." He paused. "Lived, that is, naturally. Since I entered the spirit world I've had, of course, to give up my painting. Still, I've no doubt at all that the gift is still there." He whistled softly, tilted his Balmoral bonnet and I could see he was mighty pleased with himself. As usual.

I figured I ought to say something about this point. "Pop says an artist has to be honest with himself and about his work if he wants to be a real painter."

Malcolm waved his hand impatiently. "All your father needs is a wee bit of help from someone who *knows* something about painting."

"Pop's had lessons in Hartford—"

"Hartford?" Malcolm repeated in a shocked voice. "No, Jasper, not the colonies! In Europe. I mean someone who's studied in Paris, and Amsterdam and London. Someone who has sat at the feet of the likes of Watteau and Hogarth."

I stared. "Watteau? Hogarth? I've heard Pop talk about them. But they died more than two hundred years ago!"

"Aye, that is so."

"But, gosh, Malcolm, don't you see, if they're dead *that* long nobody would be alive who—" I stopped. "You!" I gasped.

"Me." He smiled.

CHAPTER SEVEN

I was exactly one week later, and the night before the opening of the Litchville Art Show that it happened. I was watching television in the living room and Mom and Debbie were working around the kitchen with the radio going when Pop, who had just gone upstairs, came bursting out of his atelier as though shot from a cannon. His face was red and angry. Now Pop doesn't usually get red and angry. Sometimes he gets red. And sometimes he gets angry. But he seldom gets both red *and* angry, unless he's awfully mad about something, and I could see he was awfully mad about something right now as he stormed down the stairs.

"Who's been fooling with my painting!" he hollered. He glared at me. "Was it you, Jasper?"

I should explain here that whenever anything goes wrong around our house and they're not sure who did it,

I'm the first one they question. I don't think it's because I'm shifty-eyed or anything like that. I guess they just figure I somehow know more about what's going on around the house than anyone else. In the beginning I used to be flattered in a way but not any more.

"Me?" I exclaimed switching off the television. "Fooling with your painting? I'd never do a thing like that, Pop."

He scowled. "Well *somebody* did. And if it wasn't you, who was it?"

I scratched my head. It was a kind of loaded question. I mean if you eliminate me you get everybody. It didn't seem a fair match somehow.

Mom and Debbie came in from the kitchen. They must have heard Pop's voice above the radio. Mom stared at him. "What's gotten into you, Henry Trimble? Why should anyone in this house want to touch your painting?"

"That's what I want to know," he said grimly. "I wouldn't mind so much except it's the painting I've been working on all week. The one I'm entering in the Litchville Art Show tomorrow. It's too late to do it over again. Now I've got nothing to submit." He breathed hard. "If I ever find out who did it—I'll—I'll wring his neck!"

I shifted uneasily in my chair. The only two male necks in the house belonged to Pop and me. As he was

57

the one who intended to do the wringing, this narrowed the available necks down to mine.

"But nobody would do a thing like that, Daddy," Debbie said indignantly. "Even Jasper wouldn't."

"Thanks," I said.

"That's true." Mom chimed in. "Are you sure, Henry? I've noticed your eyes aren't what they used to be."

"No," snapped Pop, real sarcastic-like. "And neither are my paintings. Or at least the one I was working on last night."

Mom frowned. "It wasn't one of those abstract things, Henry, with all the lines and the mixed-up colors? It would be hard to know for sure whether somebody was touching it or not, wouldn't it?"

Pop held his head. "Look," he said with a growl. "Follow me closely. It's not an abstract. I know *exactly* what I'm painting. And what I just found on the easel upstairs wasn't what I left there last night. So somebody did it, and if it wasn't anyone in this room—" He stopped and glanced over at Debbie. "You don't think it might have been Albert? He was here last night—"

"Albert?" Debbie exclaimed in horror. "*Our* Albert?"

"Yours," I corrected.

"Well," Pop said, "all the rest of you say you didn't do it, so that leaves Albert. Nobody else has been here. Besides he's got a beard—"

"Oh, for heaven's sake, Daddy!" Debbie cut in. "So Albert has a beard! All painters don't have beards."

"That's right," I agreed helpfully. "Look at Grandma Moses and—"

"Shut up, Jasper!" Debbie said in a low, harsh voice. I guess it was really a hiss only it's hard to hiss something like "shut up."

"Henry," Mom said briskly, "we've talked about this long enough! No one here has touched your painting and that includes Albert. And if no one here touched it then you're saying that someone broke into the house while we were all sleeping, crept up to your atelier, worked on your painting, then stole out of the house again. Now that's nonsense, Henry, and you know it."

Pop shut his eyes. "Of course I know it, Clara! The whole thing's crazy!"

"It certainly is!" Mom agreed. "I've heard of cat burglars but this is the first time I've run across a cat painter. Now, either you just imagined it all, Henry, or—"

"Come!" snapped Pop as he headed for the stairs. His face was getting kind of red and angry looking again. "I've had enough of this! Look at the painting for yourself."

We all trooped behind him up the stairs with me bringing up the rear. I wasn't in any hurry as I needed all the time I could get to think. I was sure, of course, who had done the retouching of Pop's painting. Malcolm MacDhu. I had been on the point of telling Pop but something had held me back. That something was the fact that if I did tell him we had a boarder in the house who was a ghost who had studied art under Watteau and Hogarth, Pop most likely wouldn't believe me. You just don't run into boarders like that. At least not around Zip Code 06107.

Pop thrust open the door of the atelier which he had slammed shut on his way downstairs. We all gathered around him and stared at the painting on the stretched canvas square that rested on the easel. The scene showed a whitewashed farmhouse—it looked like the Bonellis' across the way—with some brown cows chewing grass in the front. There were a few white clouds too and a couple of trees. Nothing much seemed to be happening. "What's it called, Pop?" I asked.

He scowled at it. "I *had* called it *Arrangement in White and Brown*. But look at it! Someone—it had to be someone—has heightened the light coming through those trees. And see here, where the brown shadows have been deepened near the farmhouse. I never did that! I'll admit it's all rather vague and subtle but it's there just the same. And it has somehow—I'm not sure why—affected the harmony of what I was trying to achieve. Everything in a picture is supposed to balance, lines and shapes and color patterns. The gradations and the interplay of light and shadow have somehow been altered. Not much of course, still—"

He stopped, looked gloomily at the painting, and shook his head. "I had told George Pottenbaugh and the others at the Art League that I was entering it in the show tomorrow. Now I'm wondering whether I should. It's—it's not the way I *feel* about the arrangement!"

"But, Pop," I said, "I told Rocky Bonelli and some of the kids at school that you were in the show. You can't drop out now."

"Sure I can," he said grimly.

Debbie studied the canvas. "*Arrangement in White and Brown*. Mm—I kind of like it the way it is, Daddy."

"But, Debbie, look. See the shadows? How they've been emphasized? The relationship of light and dark has been upset."

Debbie shrugged. "Then call it *Arrangement in Brown and White* instead of *White and Brown*." For an older sister Debbie can be pretty smart now and then.

Pop said nothing. He kept looking at the painting. Finally he sighed. "I guess I could have been mistaken. Besides, as you say, Clara, how could anybody have gotten into the house? And if they did, why should they tamper with my painting?" He shrugged. "Very well, then, I'll go ahead and enter it tomorrow. *Arrangement in Brown and White*."

"All you can do is lose, Pop," I said. I didn't mean it that way but that's the way the words came out.

"Thanks," he said shortly. "I don't mind the losing part. I've done that often enough before. It's something else. Something that's hard to explain. Even to myself. However, let's forget all of that. I'll enter it in the show. Just as it is."

"All that fuss and feathers about nothing," Mom grumbled. "You should have known nobody would think of touching your old painting."

"It's not an old painting," Pop returned huffily. "In fact, it's so new it isn't even finished yet." He picked up a brush and quickly scrawled his name in the lower right-hand corner of the canvas. "There! Now it's finished!"

Mom and Debbie had left the atelier and I stood alongside Pop regarding the painting. "Now it's finished," he said again, only a little sadder this time and softer. Pop can get awfully wrapped up in his work—they call it something like emotional involvement—and he treats his paintings as though they were part of himself and maybe they are.

"Pop," I said, "Watteau and Hogarth, they were pretty good painters, weren't they?"

"What's that?" He smiled. "Of course. The best. Still are. Not that they had a great deal in common except that they lived around the same time. Watteau painted mostly elegantly dressed young men and women of the French court. Hogarth worked mainly with ordinary people around London, shrimp girls and servants and roistering drunkards. Why do you ask?"

"Oh, nothing much. Somebody I know happened to mention their names the other day." I closed the door. "See you around, Pop!"

A Ghost around
the house.

mostly elegantly dressed young
men and woman of the french
court. Hogart worked mainly
with ordinary people around
London. Shrimp girl and
servant and roistering drunkard
Why do you ask?

CHAPTER EIGHT

I HAD JUST brought in a load of firewood from the shed the following night when Pop came home. I knew he had been over at the Art League for he had taken *Arrangement in Brown and White* with him when he had driven off in the car that morning. Mom was attending a social at the church and Debbie was getting her hair done. Debbie's always getting her hair done. You would think that anyone who spent as much time as she did trying to look glamorous would either give up the whole business in disgust or change beauty parlors. All it's ever gotten her is Albert Hooplewaite and with prizes like that who wants to win anyway?

Pop didn't say anything when he came in. He didn't even ask if Mom or Debbie was home which wasn't like him at all. It was only after he had tossed his overcoat on a hook and sat down on his chair near the fireplace that I could see something had happened. It was hard to tell what it was for he didn't look exactly happy. For that matter he didn't look exactly sad either. He just sat and stared into the fireplace. There wasn't any expression at all on his face.

"Anything wrong, Pop?" I asked. It wasn't like him to sit and say nothing. Besides I knew he had been to the Art Show. Usually when he's been there and comes back he's pretty talkative.

I guess he hadn't heard me for I had to repeat the question in a louder voice before he suddenly looked at me with a quick start. "What? Wrong? No, nothing's wrong, Jasper." His voice was awfully quiet, though, and I could tell that if nothing was wrong, something at least was up.

It was maybe five minutes later that he spoke again. He said, "*Arrangement in Brown and White*. It won, Jasper."

I was splicing tape on the cassette recorder that Mom had given me last Christmas and I almost stabbed myself with the scissors I was holding. "It what?" I gasped.

"It won," he said simply. He looked at me as though I were a stranger. "First Prize."

For a long moment I said nothing, too stunned to talk. It was impossible. Pop had never won a First Prize. Pop had never won anything, not even an Honorable Mention. And here he had walked off with the top award for a painting he hadn't even wanted to show! "Gosh, Pop!" I finally exclaimed. "That's terrific! That proves Malcolm—" I stopped and choked back the rest of the words I was about to say.

He looked at me curiously. "Malcolm? Who's Malcolm?"

I felt my face go warm. No sense in trying to tell Pop about the ghost. At least not now. Not after Pop had finally come through as a winner. Nobody had ever worked harder for success than he had. It would have been a rotten trick now to come out and tell him that it wasn't Henry Trimble who had won the prize but a ghost named Malcolm MacDhu.

"Oh nothing, Pop," I mumbled. I plunged ahead before he could say anything. "First Prize! Gosh. I just can't believe it!"

"Neither can I," he said drily, tugging at his chin. "The judges kept telling me what a fine picture it was. Best thing I had ever done. One of them raved about the bewitched mood I had captured. Another thought it had a rare ethereal quality about it."

"Ethereal?" I repeated. I learned a long time ago that you can get yourself tagged as pretty stupid if you go around all the time asking what certain words mean. Now I simply repeat the word letting my voice climb up it so that it comes out higher at the end than the front.

Sometimes, of course, people misunderstand and think you're some kind of nutty Swiss yodeler but at least they don't think you're stupid. And usually they automatically explain the word without thinking about it, which is the general idea in the first place.

"Airy," Pop mused, as though talking to himself. "A sense of other-worldliness. As though in some indefinable way the cows and the farm were gently floating in space. None of the judges could explain exactly what the haunting quality was that they felt in the picture and it seemed to puzzle them as much as it puzzled me. But they loved it." He groped in his jacket for his pipe. "Ethereal."

"Most ethereal painting I ever did see," I said.

He nodded, then got to his feet without lighting his pipe. "I'll pick up your Mother and Debbie. You get to work on that history assignment. I shouldn't be too long." He shrugged on his coat and stood lost in thought for a moment. "Ethereal," he murmured again before closing the door behind him.

I waited for the sound of the car to die away before dashing upstairs to break the news to Malcolm. I burst into his room. It was empty and I was just about to look elsewhere when I noticed that the rocking chair by the window was swaying gently. "Malcolm!" I exclaimed. "Is that you in the empty chair?"

"It could hardly be empty if I'm in it," snapped a

familiar voice. "Just a minute, lad, and I'll be with you." There was a pause, then from the space above the chair Malcolm's voice came again, a grumbling note to it. "It's that confounded, idiotic central heating you have around here! It dries out my ectoplasm! Never had any trouble at Strowan Castle." It took a few minutes before a wraithlike figure started to materialize near the window. The image gradually sharpened into the familiar features and form of Malcolm MacDhu. He looked a little paler than usual and I could see he was upset about something. He peered nervously over my shoulder in the direction of the door. "She is no' around?"

I glanced back. "Who, Malcolm?"

"Your mother."

"My mother?" I looked at him in astonishment. "She's out at a social in the church. What's the matter with you, Malcolm?"

"She's out?" He let out a long sigh of relief. "Well, and thank the good Lord for that! She and that big beast she drags around on a leash."

I stared. Poor Malcolm! He must have really flipped. Maybe the central heating had affected more than his ectoplasm. I said, "But Malcolm, we don't have any big beasts in the house. All we've got is Cleo, our cat, and she doesn't have a leash."

"I'm no' talking at all about the cat! I'm talking about

68

that fierce one your mother takes along with her through the house! Sniffing at the floor, after me, like a blood-hound, and letting out that inhuman wail of his like a banshee with the horrors, no less! Aye, and it's enough to frighten a ghost half to life it is for certain."

It took me a few minutes to figure out what he was talking about. Suddenly the light broke and I grinned. "Now don't tell me, Malcolm, you're afraid of Mom's vacuum cleaner?"

"It's no' a bloodhound?"

I shook my head. "A dusthound maybe. Every house has one."

"We had none in Strowan Castle," he said coldly. "And a good thing too." He looked at me suspiciously. "What does she use it for?"

"Why to pick up dirt, Malcolm. It's what we call a labor saving device."

He frowned again. "That big iron ball we saw. The one they are using to knock down the castle. Was that one, too?"

"One what, Malcolm?"

"A labor saving thing?"

"I suppose you might call it that. Without the wrecker's ball it would take a lot longer to knock down the castle."

His lips tightened in a thin, hard line. "I'm no' caring

much for those devices. Besides, what happens to all the labor that is saved? Doesn't anybody work anymore?"

"Of course they do, Malcolm. Everybody works as much if not more than he ever did."

He shrugged. "So the whole thing is plain daft! If everybody will be working as you say, you haven't really saved any labor now, have you?"

"I suppose so, I mean if you put it that way," I agreed doubtfully. It was hard to follow Malcolm's reasoning sometimes. "Of course with everyone working faster we get a lot of things done we'd never be able to do otherwise."

"Aye," he said bitterly, "like destroying old castles. Anyway, let us talk no more of this. I am curious about the painting your father had in the room next door. I looked for it a wee while ago and it was gone."

"*Arrangement in Brown and White?*" I smiled. "Of course. Pop took it to the Litchville Art Show."

"Art Show? You mean, Jasper, he entered our—that is, his—picture?"

I nodded and grinned.

"But—" He hesitated for a moment and there was a crafty look in his eyes. He seemed to be waiting for me to speak and when I didn't he strolled over to the mirror, kilt swaying, and studied himself. I knew he was also studying me in the glass. "And what happened?" he asked carelessly.

"*Arrangement in Brown and White* took First Prize."

"Well!" Malcolm's breath came out soft and slow. "So we won, eh?" He seemed vastly pleased with himself and I could see he had eyes only for himself now as he smiled into the mirror. Quite clearly the son of the chief of all the MacDhus of Gilnochie was his old self again.

"I told you, did I no', that I was something of a painter? Clearly my hand has lost none of its cunning after all these years. I saw at once what was wrong with the picture and I only did what I could to help." He sighed. "Och, and if only I had lived a wee bit longer! What immortal art might have left my brush! Why is it that the gifted are struck down so early in life? Keats and Burns and Chopin." He struck a melancholy pose but I could see he was tickled silly at how things had gone.

He glanced down at his fingers. "Your father, he is happy of course?"

I hesitated. "I'm not sure."

"Not sure?" Malcolm was plainly astonished. "But did you no' tell me he had never won anything before?"

I nodded.

"But—but I'm no' understanding, Jasper! I have made him famous around Litchville and Wethersfield. Why is no' the man happy?"

"It's not that he isn't happy, Malcolm. He didn't say he

71

wasn't. He just seemed kind of, well, stunned about it all."

"Well, that's reasonable enough," Malcolm said. "If someone like Michelangelo had helped me with one of my paintings I would have been stunned myself." He paused. "No' that I'm as good as Michelangelo, mind you. I wouldn't want you to think that."

I grinned. You just couldn't get mad at Malcolm MacDhu! Maybe he had been a pretty good painter, just as he had claimed to be, but it certainly took an awfully big tablespoonful of gall to even link your name with that of Michelangelo! Yes, and not to mention those of Keats and Burns and Chopin. But modesty was never one of Malcolm's strong suits anyway, which come to think of it, was the reason why old Calum Carnoustie had laid that curse on him in the first place.

He rubbed his hands together and whistled softly. Plainly some pleasant thought had just struck him. I wasn't kept long in doubt as to what it was. "When is the next Art Show, Jasper?"

"November 20, in Greenlawn." I looked at him. "Why?"

His dark eyes gleamed mischievously. "And your father will be entering it?"

"Of course. Pop never misses one around here. Now that he's won in Litchville it just makes sense that he enter the Greenlawn showing. After all, he's a teacher. It's bound to help him at the college."

"So then he will be starting on another painting?"

I nodded. "He always likes to enter something new. Pop goes through a lot of Periods, you know. He's had a Blue Period, and a Green Period. He even had a Blue and Green Period once."

"But never a Winning Period, eh, Jasper?" Malcolm smiled. "That is, until now." He suddenly glanced down at his feet and I noticed they were no longer visible.

"Your feet, Malcolm!" I cried. "They're gone!"

"It's that daft central heating again! Upsets the ecto-plasm. Well, never mind. I have to do some thinking about the new painting and I always think better when I'm no' visible. It's better for the gray cells." He chuckled. "That's a joke."

"It is?" I asked doubtfully.

"And don't worry at all about that Greenlawn Show on November 20."

"I'm not."

"Good." Only half of him was visible now and the outlines of his face were fading. The feather on his Balmoral bonnet was already floating in space. "Jasper, have you ever heard tell of a ghost writer?"

I nodded. "That's someone who writes for someone else. Why?"

73

"Och nothing! Nothing at all. I was just thinking of something." He chuckled again.

"What?"

The head was gone but the voice came from the space where it had been a moment ago. "Henry Trimble will be the first artist in history to have had his own ghost painter!"

CHAPTER NINE

I GUESS, come to think of it, no painter who ever lived had such a sudden climb to fame and success as my Pop. One moment he had been a nobody, an amateur who couldn't have sold a painting if he had been working overtime in Macy's Art Department. The next, people from all over Connecticut were knocking down our door to buy Henry Trimble's paintings. I don't have to tell you that he took First Prize at the Greenlawn show. Or that he did the same in Simsbury. And West Hartford. And Farmington. In fact, for the next three months there wasn't an art show around Connecticut that Pop didn't enter and win. And the critics couldn't get enough. They kept saying things like how Pop had an uncanny feeling for the supernatural. How they found in his paintings a brooding sense of timelessness, an aura of haunting and all pervading melancholy. I never could find all these things there when *I* looked, but then I don't look like any of the critics I know. Which may be just as well.

Of course, I was pretty puffed up about Pop and the way things had worked out. After all, he had been teaching art at the Litchville Community College for years and I knew that deep down it had bothered him that he had never gotten anyplace with his paintings. When you think about it, when a guy's teaching other people how to paint, you figure he'd be able to do it himself. I've learned, though, that it doesn't work out that way. Most teachers can only teach and Pop says some of them don't even do that. Anyway it was great seeing Pop, who's the finest guy in the world, suddenly hailed on all sides as a brilliant craftsman.

On the other hand I was pretty proud of Malcolm too. Sure he was just about the vainest, most conceited character I had ever met, but you couldn't say he didn't deliver at the plate, or maybe I should say, the easel. Looking back, I suppose he probably *had* been the best horseman around Gilnochie, just like he said. It must have jarred his ego even worse than the rest of him when he landed on the ground from the back of old Jenny, that fateful day in 1720.

And of course he was tickled pink, or maybe I should say, pale, every time I told him that Pop had won another show or sold another painting. He kept rubbing his hands gleefully and strutting up and down in his kilt, or admiring himself in the mirror. "Your father is coming along just grand," he would exclaim, "just grand indeed."

But if Malcolm MacDhu was delighted about the way things were going, Pop wasn't. The more famous he became, the gloomier he got. It really bugged me. You'd think, wouldn't you, that he would have been doing handsprings over finally reaching the top of the ladder. But not Pop. In fact, he had looked a lot happier and more content when he had been a failure than he looked now that he was a success. Even a big feature story in the Hartford *Courant*, under the heading *"Litchville Painter Hailed as Modern El Greco,"* failed to lift up his spirits. I cornered him in his atelier the morning after the story came out determined to get to the bottom of the mystery.

"Look, Pop, I don't get it. All your life you've been knocking yourself out to get just one of your pictures sold and now you can't keep up with the demand. You win every art show you enter. The critics are raving about you. So what goes with the long face? It's driving me nuts!"

He smiled and ruffled my hair. "Sorry, Jasper. I guess I've not been too easy to live with lately. Maybe it's all this publicity." He glanced down at the headlines in the *Courant*. *"Litchville Painter Hailed as Modern El Greco."* He tossed the paper aside. "I don't want to be El Greco! I just want to be Henry Trimble!"

I stared. "But you are!"

"I am?" he returned grimly. "I wonder. One thing I

77

do know. Those paintings that are signed Henry Trimble weren't done by Henry Trimble. Oh, some parts of them were. But I know my own work. And those paintings that have been winning all the prizes weren't done by me."

"But what difference does it make, Pop? I mean, so what?"

"So what? I'll tell you so what. I may not be a talented painter but at least I hope I'm an honest one!"

"But, gosh, if nobody knows—"

"*I* know," he said quietly. He hesitated. "Maybe all of this will seem awfully square to you, Jasper, but I'd rather be a failure on my own terms than a success on someone else's. Maybe I'm just a thick-headed Connecticut Yankee but I happen to believe that art is an expression of truth. And what I'm signing—" He did not finish the sentence.

I didn't say anything. I had been on the point of telling him about Malcolm but thought it better to keep my mouth shut. At least for the time being. I was still kind of hoping Pop would get over his scruples. He had worked hard all his life and deserved a break. Besides, who was going to know? Only Malcolm and I knew the secret. Still, there it was. Perhaps Pop, no less than Malcolm MacDhu, had his pride. Yes, perhaps that was it.

"What I can't figure," he said thoughtfully, "is how

it's being done. Ever since that first incident I've been locking the door to the atelier and I'm the only one with a key. So how does he get into the room?"

I knew all right but I was sure Pop would never believe me. You have to believe in ghosts to know that closed doors don't mean a thing to them. Especially when they're non-materialized, which Malcolm usually is to save his ectoplasm. I sometimes wonder whether other ghosts are as frugal with their ectoplasm as Malcolm is with his. Maybe coming from Scotland he's just a little more careful about how he uses it.

"Of course," continued Pop, glancing out of the window, "somebody might be able to scramble up that old oak tree out there. See how its branches just about reach the window sill here? He would have to be awfully light and agile, though."

"Could be a monkey," I suggested.

He looked kind of startled. "What?"

"A monkey. Monkeys can climb trees all right and some of them can paint. I was reading just the other day in the Hartford *Times* where somebody entered a painting done by a monkey in an abstract art show in Kansas City, and you know what? It won First Prize. Maybe we've got some crazy monkey loose in the neighborhood with a yen for art. He can't enter a show himself so—"

"Shut up, Jasper," Pop cut in. "The whole thing doesn't make sense. Why should one painter want to tamper with another painter's work? If he's so good why doesn't he submit his own work? Why does he fool around with mine?"

I tried to think of something that would help both Pop and Malcolm. "Maybe he needs you, Pop. Maybe you need him too. I mean the two of you could be one of those natural teams like Barnum and Bailey or Gilbert and Sullivan, or—"

"Jasper, please!" Pop said wearily. He frowned and stared moodily out of the window as though lost in thought.

"Are you lost in thought, Pop?" I inquired after a long silence.

"Yes. There's something I wonder about. This—this mysterious collaborator of mine—why does everything he paints have such a sense of—of remoteness? One might say of the supernatural? Muted, swirling eddies of mist and vapor. Horizons fading into infinity. A sense of overwhelming loss and melancholy." He was silent again. Finally he shrugged. "Anyway, after tonight it won't make any difference."

"What do you mean, Pop?"

"Just this. I've had enough of whatever is going on around here. More than enough. Albert Hooplewaite has agreed to lend me Wolfgang, that big German shepherd dog of his. He'll be sleeping in the atelier tonight.

That should put an end to all this hanky-panky that's been going on for the last few weeks."

I felt my jaws collapse in horror as a vision of Albert's huge dog flashed across my mind. Wolfgang was the biggest and fiercest dog in the neighborhood. He had a real mean disposition too. The Hooplewaites were the only family that picked up its letters at the post office. The mailman simply refused to make deliveries when Wolfgang was around.

"Wolfgang," I said dully, "he's going to be sleeping here?"

Pop nodded cheerfully. "Right in this room."

"But, Pop!" I cried in alarm, "what's going to happen to—" I choked back the name I had almost spoken.

"—To my mysterious collaborator?" Pop chuckled. "Jasper, I couldn't care less. All I'm concerned about is that I'm free once again to paint as *I* want to paint. I don't know what's been going on around here, but after tonight with Wolfgang on the premises, it will be all over." He let out a soft sigh of satisfaction and picked up his palette knife.

"Should be quite a lively evening, Jasper," he murmured. "Quite a lively evening!"

CHAPTER TEN

I T WAS. In fact it turned out to be just about the liveliest
anybody in the Trimble clan could remember. And
that took in all the other Trimbles in Massachusetts,
New Hampshire, Vermont and Maine.

It started out quietly enough. Albert came over around
eight with Wolfgang in tow. Actually Wolfgang was in
front, straining at his leash, so I suppose really the one
in tow was Albert. For once he seemed happy—I'm talking about Albert—and I guess he was kind of looking forward to whatever was going to take place that night.
Wolfgang, his hair bristling, his ugly fangs bared,
seemed even meaner than usual, which wasn't easy if you
happen to look like Wolfgang normally looks.

I wanted to warn Malcolm of what was going to happen but never did get the chance. After delivering the
evening papers, Mom had me clean out the garage and
stack firewood. When supper was finished, Pop kept me
pretty close to my homework so that by the time I finally

got to bed Albert had already taken Wolfgang up to the atelier.

More than once as I lay wide awake in my room, the thought flashed across my mind that if I slipped quietly out of bed I could still warn Malcolm of what was waiting for him in the atelier. Each time the thought came my flesh went cold as I remembered the huge brute waiting in the darkness in the room above where I lay. Almost certainly he would hear me as I crept upstairs. Albert used to boast that Wolfgang's hearing was so good he could pick up the sound of a butterfly landing on a bowl of creamed marshmallows. I mean that dog had *ears*.

I felt sick and no matter how I tried I couldn't sleep. I kept tossing and turning and thinking of Malcolm, and the dog waiting for him in the atelier. Poor Malcolm! He wouldn't have a chance! I don't know how fast a ghost can run but I'd have been willing to bet that an all time world's record was about to be set that night in Litchville, Connecticut. I was still lying in bed, staring miserably into the darkness above my head, every nerve taut and quivering, when it happened. One moment everything had been as quiet as a grave. The next the silence was shattered by an ascending inhuman scream that made the hairs bristle on the back of my neck. The scream was followed a couple of seconds later by the sound of a wooden door shattering, then by a violent series of dull thuds as some heavy object came hurtling down the stairs. The unholy hammering on the stairs was succeeded the next moment by a splintering of glass from the kitchen. Then silence.

I had never felt so miserable in all my life as I did at that moment. Poor Malcolm! Where would he go to now? Homeless, frightened out of his wits, with no one to turn to. And it was all my fault. Ashamed of the cowardice that had kept me shivering with fright in the dark, I leaped out of bed and switched on the light. There was hollering now from the bedroom next door and I knew Pop was up. Then I heard Mom's voice, and then Debbie's. We all met in the corridor, white-faced and shaken. It was Pop in his pajamas, my baseball bat in his hand, who switched on the light and led the charge upstairs. He stopped so short at the top that we all crashed into him and for a moment all four of us were in danger of toppling back down the way we had just come. Pop clutched me with his free hand and I grabbed Debbie who clung for dear life to Mom. Only when we had regained our balance did I spot the reason for Pop's sudden halt.

The door to the atelier was half open, shattered and pitched over on its hinges. There were pieces of splintered wood on the carpet and a few tufts of coarse hair. Through the half-open door I could see that the atelier was empty. Everything was in place, just as Pop had left it before going to bed. The only thing not in place was the huge shepherd dog that Pop had brought in to protect his paintings. Wolfgang was gone.

I suppose it must have taken me a good minute before I finally realized what had happened. I breathed a long low sigh of relief. It hadn't been Malcolm who had come hurtling down the stairs and broken the kitchen window in his panic to flee the house. It had been Wolfgang! Wolfgang, the toughest, meanest brute in the neighborhood, terrorized out of his skin by a ghost. I grinned. I should have known better than to have worried about Malcolm MacDhu. Anybody who knew how to handle horses almost certainly knew how to handle dogs. And of course poor Wolfgang's past experience had been restricted solely to milkmen and mailmen. This was his first meeting with a real dead ghost. And judging from the way he had departed through the kitchen window, I figured it was probably his last.

On the way downstairs I lingered behind the others, then cut back and darted into Malcolm's room. I switched on the light. There was nobody there, then I noticed the rocking chair was gently swaying.

"Malcolm," I whispered, "is that you, Malcolm?"

"Of course it's me," snapped a familiar voice from somewhere above the moving chair. "Who did you think it was? Wolfgang?"

"I see you've met," I said.

"Aye, briefly. I heard your father mention his name. Horrible name. Wouldn't wish it on—on a dog."

"What happened?"

"Och, and I'm no' knowing at all, Jasper! I just glided over to pat him on the head and the next thing you know he let out this horrible scream and through the closed door he went." He sighed. "Not a friendly beast I'm afraid. But then of course he didn't know me."

I chuckled. "He will the next time. *If* there's a next time." I was beginning to feel a little foolish speaking into an empty room and I said, "Aren't you going to materialize, Malcolm?"

"Can't. Used up all my ectoplasm on Wolfgang. I was thinking he would not often be meeting a ghost so I wanted to give him a special treat. I'm afraid maybe I overdid the pale green a wee bit. Almost scared myself when I looked into the mirror." There was a dry chuckle. "Anyway, now that Wolfgang's gone your father and I can go back to work on our next painting."

I shifted uneasily. "Pop's getting awfully upset."

The chair suddenly stopped rocking. "And why now should *he* get upset? I've made him famous, have I no'?"

I nodded. "The only thing is, Pop doesn't care whether he's famous or not."

"The man's daft then! Everybody wants to be famous, to have other folk talk about them! It's only natural to feel that you're better than the rest."

86

"Not Pop. Not unless he's the reason why he's famous and even then it wouldn't matter to him. He's funny that way."

I heard a sniff from somewhere near the window.

"Humbug! And after all I've done for him, too!" He paused, then said in a kind of hurt voice, "It's no' easy at all working every night in the dark with just a phosphorescent glow to show you what you're painting! And it uses up my ectoplasm at a horrible rate. Aye, that's gratitude for you!"

"Sorry, Malcolm," I said. "But Pop's just that way. He's got this thing about being true to yourself. Sometimes I'm not sure I get it. Anyway, I'm glad nothing happened to you tonight. I wanted to tell you about Albert's dog but didn't get the chance."

"So that was Albert's dog, was it now? Well, well. Think no more of it, Jasper." The rocking chair was moving again and Malcolm seemed his old self when he spoke. "Your father should be starting on his new picture soon, eh, lad?"

"For the Hartford show. It's one of the biggest in the state."

"Well, and isn't that grand now! He will be quite the hero if he wins, will he no'?"

I nodded at the space above the gently bobbing chair where I supposed Malcolm to be. "He's the favorite. Everybody in the Litchville Art League expects him to win. If he does, it will be the first time that anyone from Litchville ever won at Hartford."

Malcolm's voice was a soft purr. "Then I'm thinking we must no' disappoint them, lad! Now off to bed with you! Before your father comes up and finds you talking to a rocking chair!"

CHAPTER ELEVEN

WE WERE still having breakfast the next morning, a Saturday, when the front bell rang. It was Albert. And he looked awfully peevish.

"What happened to Wolfgang last night? He's a mess!"

"You mean it just happened last night?" I asked.

"Shut up, Jasper," Pop said crossly. He glanced up from his coffee at Albert. "Frankly, I can't tell you exactly what did happen, Albert. All I know is we heard a scream from the atelier. The next moment the door smashed open and there was a horrible thumping on the stairs. Right after that there was a crash of splintering glass as something heavy went through the kitchen window. When I got to the atelier, Wolfgang was gone."

"Poor Wolfgang," Debbie said, "is he all right?"

Albert scowled. "Outside of a dislocated shoulder, a sprained leg, two broken ribs and a mass of cuts and bruises, he never looked better! What happened anyway? I know Wolfgang. Nothing scares him. He can lick twice his weight in wildcats. He's never run away from anything in his life."

Pop hesitated, as though searching for the right words. "That's what was queer about it all. There was nothing in the room when we got there. Absolutely nothing. The stairs were empty too. So was the room next to the atelier."

Albert frowned over the top of his glasses. "What about the window in the atelier, Mr. Trimble?"

"Locked. I've been locking it for the past week."

Albert glowered. "But this is crazy! If the room was empty, the window locked and nobody passed you on the stairs, what happened to Wolfgang?"

I said, "A dislocated shoulder, a sprained leg, two broken ribs—"

"Do shut up, Jasper," Debbie said wearily. "Albert's right. *Something* had to frighten Wolfgang."

"Nothing frightens Wolfgang," Albert corrected firmly. "He's got the heart of a lion."

I was all set to make a crack about him also having the feet of a gazelle, but held my tongue. Albert looked mighty sore and there was no sense in getting him sorer. He asked Pop if he could look around upstairs just to see if there was any clue as to what might have happened.

Pop shrugged. "Go ahead."

Albert was gone for about five minutes. He was

unusually quiet when he came back to the living room.

"See anything?" Mom asked as she poured him a cup of coffee.

Albert shook his head slowly. "No, nothing." He hesitated for a moment. "By the way, when did you get that crazy rocking chair, Mr. Trimble?"

Mom looked at him curiously. "You mean the one in the room next to the atelier? We've always had it, Albert. Why?"

Again he hesitated. "Oh nothing, I suppose. Seemed to be moving when I came out of the atelier. As though someone had just been rocking in it."

Debbie shook her head. "No one's been upstairs since breakfast, Albert."

"Must have been a current of air," Pop said.

Albert nodded doubtfully. "I suppose you're right, Mr. Trimble. Just kind of shook me for a moment. Swaying back and forth for all the world as though there was someone sitting in it." He gulped his coffee down and got up. "Have to be getting home. See you later, Debbie." He stopped when he opened the door, then frowned back at the stairs. "Air current," he said moodily. "It had to be!"

I had been hoping that after the Wolfgang incident Pop would somehow snap out of his glum mood and get back to the business of being his old cheerful self. Two days passed, then three, but Pop if anything grew more silent and withdrawn. He didn't even seem to want to talk about painting. He'd just sit around the house and scowl whenever anyone mentioned what a big hit he was. It got so he wouldn't even go to the phone when people called up asking to buy his pictures.

"Idiots!" he growled one afternoon after a flurry of such calls, "where were all these people hiding during the last ten years? I needed their encouragement then, not now!"

I shrugged. "Remember, Pop. You weren't a success then."

He nodded bitterly. "That's right, Jasper. I wasn't a success then. But I am now. I am Gauguin after he arrived in Tahiti. I am suddenly respected as a brilliant new force. But all the time I'm a fake. An impostor—" He kind of swallowed and didn't say any more.

He looked so miserable, slumped over on the sofa that I could hold the words back no longer. "Pop," I said, "I didn't tell you before because I thought you wouldn't believe me. Besides I wanted to be extra proud of you, and have everyone talk about you, you being my Pop and all, and the greatest guy in the world."

He didn't say anything. He just looked at me, waiting. I took a deep, deep breath.

"Pop!" I blurted out, "the one who's been helping you

with the pictures is Malcolm! He studied art in London and Paris too. That's why he's so good. And—"

"Malcolm? Malcolm who?"

"Malcolm MacDhu. He's a ghost and—"

"A what?"

"A ghost."

Pop nodded calmly. Too calmly. "I see. A ghost."

"He moved in with us when they started to knock down Strowan Castle to make room for the new high rise apartments. He came over from Scotland with the castle and he's been a ghost for two hundred and fifty years. He wears a kilt and his father was the chief of all the Mac-Dhus of Gilnochie."

Pop cradled his head between his hands as though he was praying. Maybe he was. Finally he looked up. "Jasper, please! Maybe you're just trying to cheer me up, but remember one thing. Nobody believes in ghosts anymore! Not even ghosts that come from Gil—Gil—"

"Gilnochie," I finished. "But if it wasn't a ghost that frightened Wolfgang, what was it? You saw for yourself that there was nobody upstairs. And the window was locked too."

"That's true," he said slowly. "I've been doing a lot of thinking about that. There was nothing, absolutely nothing up there. And I'm sure no one could have gotten down the stairs without my seeing him. The only possible explanation I've been able to come up with is that Wolfgang had a nightmare of some kind."

"The nightmare was Malcolm," I said. "Besides what about your paintings? Isn't it true that whoever was working on them always did it at night when everyone was asleep?"

"Yes—but—"

"See, Pop? Who else but a ghost prowls around at night? And who else but a ghost could go through a locked door? And finally anyone retouching your painting in the dark would need a light, wouldn't he? But a ghost now, a ghost like Malcolm MacDhu, all he'd have to do would be to turn up his ectoplasm!"

Pop stared at me wonderingly. "Ectoplasm?" He looked away and I could see he was pretty shaken. He seemed to be talking to himself. "*Ethereal* that was the word they used. *A sense of other-worldliness. Of fantasy.* . . ." His face suddenly hardened. "Nonsense! The whole thing's idiotic! A two hundred and fifty year old ghost who paints!"

I said, "So what, Pop? It's no harder to believe in a two hundred and fifty year old ghost who paints than in a two hundred and fifty year old ghost who *doesn't* paint."

His face got red. "I didn't say I believed—" He swallowed hard. "Okay, okay. I know it's nonsense, but nonsense or not, you've helped me make up my mind, Jasper! I'm calling up George Pottenbaugh at the Art League and telling him the truth!"

"What truth?"

He sucked in his breath as he reached for the phone. "That somebody other than Henry Trimble has been painting all those prize winning pictures around here!"

CHAPTER TWELVE

I OPENED the door twenty minutes later and let in Mr. Pottenbaugh.

In addition to being president of the Litchville Art League, Mr. Pottenbaugh is also active in a lot of other projects around our village. In fact, come to think about it, there's hardly a project around Litchville that Mr. Pottenbaugh *isn't* in. Mom says he's the most civic-minded person we've got in Litchville and that we should be grateful we have him. Mr. Pottenbaugh is a huge man with a huge voice to match and when he talks all his teeth show.

"Dad in, Jasper?" he boomed. He didn't wait for me to say anything and by the time I had hung up his coat he was already in the living room talking to Pop.

"What's up, Henry? Got your call just as I was on my way to the Rotary. It can wait. Something about your painting I understand, Henry? Want you to know you're doing a terrific job! Yes sir, Henry, a terrific job! Litchville is mighty proud of you! Mighty proud indeed. Said to my wife just before I left, 'Mark my words, Penelope, Henry Trimble is going to put lil' ol' Litchville on the map yet!' Yes sir! That's the exact words I used and I meant every last one of them. When we—that is, you, Henry—walk off with the big Connecticut Academy show in Hartford next week you can bet that Litchville is gonna really be proud of its native son!" He stopped, and took a deep breath.

"Thanks," said Pop.

Mr. Pottenbaugh pressed Pop's arm. "As president of the Art League, Henry, I don't have to tell you that I'm gonna be leaning heavily on you in the next few days. Mighty heavily."

"George," Pop said, "I've got something to tell you."

Mr. Pottenbaugh's teeth started to show but before he could say anything Pop hurried on. "About those paintings, George. The ones that have been winning all the awards. They're not mine."

For once Mr. Pottenbaugh was speechless. He stared for maybe twenty seconds. "They're not yours?" he asked finally.

Pop nodded.

"But—but—" exclaimed Mr. Pottenbaugh in a shocked kind of voice, "do you mean to say you submitted paintings done by someone else and pretended they were yours?"

Again Pop nodded and struck the bowl of his pipe against his cupped hand. "That's about how it figures, George," he said calmly. "Got a match?"

Mr. Pottenbaugh ignored the question. His heavy face was a turnip purple. "That's about how it figures?" he repeated. "You perpetrate a fraud that is going to reflect on everyone in the Litchville Art League, including its president, and that's all you have to say?"

Pop shrugged. "Oh, I guess I could say a lot more, George, only what's the use? I wasn't exactly sure at first what *was* happening to my paintings."

"Except that all of a sudden they were winning," Mr. Pottenbaugh snapped.

"Right," Pop agreed. "That's when I really started to get suspicious."

Mr. Pottenbaugh eyed him glumly. "That's when I should have started getting suspicious too. Look, Henry, we've always been friends. I don't know what could have gotten into you to pull a dumb stunt like this, but what on earth are we gonna do? When word of this gets out around Litchville, all hell's gonna break loose."

Pop tapped his teeth with his pipe and nodded. "It's not going to be pleasant, George."

Mr. Pottenbaugh glowered at him. "You can say that again, only don't bother." He handed a book of matches over to Pop and said nothing for maybe two minutes which was probably some kind of record for him, I guess.

Actually he isn't such a bad sort and I kind of felt sorry for him. I had never seen anyone look quite so unhappy. I didn't feel sorry for Pop though. In fact, I had never felt quite so proud of him as I did then. It had taken courage to tell his story to Mr. Pottenbaugh. It would take more courage to face the neighbors when the news got around. But that was Pop. I shouldn't have been surprised.

Mr. Pottenbaugh suddenly seemed to think of something. "You haven't told me yet who the real painter is?"

Pop hesitated then glanced over at me. He shrugged. "What difference does it make? Let's just call him Malcolm. Malcolm MacDhu."

"Let's—just—call—him—" Mr. Pottenbaugh stuttered. "And just who, pray tell me, is Malcolm MacDhu?"

"A ghost."

"A which?"

"A ghost. His father was chief of all the MacDhus of Gilnochie."

"Oh," said Mr. Pottenbaugh.

"Jasper here tells me he's been a ghost for two hundred and fifty years. Came over from Scotland with Strowan Castle. Wears a kilt I understand."

Mr. Pottenbaugh nodded, dazed. "A kilt. Of course. I mean he has to wear *something*."

"Especially in New England," Pop said.

Mr. Pottenbaugh seemed to have recovered himself.

He squinted suspiciously at Pop. "Look, Henry, I don't know what your little game is but let's get one thing straight. Nobody believes in ghosts! And especially ghosts running around in kilts! And if nobody believes in ghosts who is gonna believe this cock-and-bull story of yours?" He looked vastly relieved as he got to his feet and eyed his watch. "Had me going there for a little while, Henry. Ghosts, eh?" He grinned. "I'm just happy it's nothing worse. So long, Henry. Can't keep the Rotary waiting." He stopped at the door and darted a glance back over his shoulder. "And by the way, that picture you're working on for the big Connecticut Academy Show next week, it's got to be your best, Henry! What was the name of that ghost again? Oh yes, Malcolm." Mr. Pottenbaugh chuckled. "That was it, Malcolm Mac-Dhu of Gilnochie." Mr. Pottenbaugh was still chuckling as he closed the door behind him.

Mr. Pottenbaugh must have told the story at the Rotary, or perhaps it had gotten around through Rocky Bonelli. I had been keeping Rocky posted on what was going on, although he still found it hard to believe that we had a ghost around the house. Anyway, it was only a few days after Mr. Pottenbaugh's visit that the local newspaper got word of the story. A girl reporter came to the house and took some pictures of the atelier and asked a lot of questions. After that there was a whole series of articles in the papers, all of them meant to be funny, I guess, although I couldn't see an awful lot in them that was really worth laughing about. One story was headlined *"Spirited Controversy rages—Is Two Hundred and Fifty Year Old Ghost Back In Old Haunts?"* Another read *"Phantom Painter Strokes Again."* There was even one that bannered *"Local Painter Wins By A 'Shade'."* I tell you it was all pretty horrible.

Things really got out of hand, though, when the local television station called up and asked if we'd mind if they programmed something called a Ghost-In at our house. It seemed they had some idea that there would be a lot of interest in setting up cameras throughout the house and catching the ghost as he took his evening stroll. They even had a sponsor picked out for the show— Higglebottom's Vanishing Cream—the Last Wrinkle in Beauty Aid. Pop had got really mad about this point and I remember he yelled something to Mom about "Ghost–In—Henry Trimble–out!" In a way I was kind of sorry Malcolm never got on television. I'll bet he would have been real good, considering some of the shows we've been seeing lately. Anyway, as far as Pop was concerned, he was getting sick and tired of the whole thing. Nobody really wanted to believe him and they treated the whole thing as a big joke or some kind of kooky publicity stunt for his pictures, which made Pop all the madder.

Of course I kept Malcolm up to date on everything that was happening. I don't have to tell you he was getting a huge charge out of it. He was proud as a peacock too, at all the publicity he was getting and kept strutting up and down in his kilt and admiring himself in the mirror. I tell you I never met anyone so conceited as Malcolm MacDhu, although maybe you have to make allowances for his being the only son of the chief of all the MacDhus of Gilnochie.

"Och, now," he exclaimed one afternoon in his room, "And isn't it just marvelous, lad? To think that everyone is talking about me—" He seemed to think of something, for suddenly he frowned and darted a quick look at me. "You did no' tell them the bit about falling off the old horse?" he asked anxiously.

I shook my head.

He let his breath out slowly. "Good, lad. I would no' want that story to get around. Even over here in America."

"Nobody knows," I said.

He rubbed his hands together in satisfaction. "And they think I'm quite the grand painter, eh? To think that after all those years I'm finally recognized as the artist I am! Fame has come late in the lives of many

102

famous men in history, Jasper, but I'm thinking it never came later into any life than it has into mine! Two hundred and fifty years!"

"Of course, Malcolm," I said doubtfully, "you have to remember that the newspapers treat the whole thing as something of a joke. They still think my father——"

Malcolm stopped me with a lordly wave of his hand. "Please, Jasper. Although I like your father it is clear enough that his talent is a humble one, at best. It is also clear that without my—er—cooperation he would still be an unknown art teacher." He suddenly paused, a curious look in his dark eyes. "There will be one thing I'll no' be understanding, though, one thing that puzzles me."

"And what is that?"

"Why, now, did your father tell this Mr. Pottenbaugh about me? It doesn't make sense at all. Everyone was praising him as the real painter. Why did the man tell them about me?"

I wasn't sure Malcolm would understand. I wasn't sure I understood myself. The words weren't easy to speak. "Because that's the way Pop is, I guess. He just felt he shouldn't take credit for something he hadn't done."

Malcolm stared at me, bewilderment in his eyes.

"But what's the difference, lad? Nobody would ever know!"

"Only Pop. He knew." I hesitated. "Maybe you don't

know Pop. It's not that he's preachy or expects other people to feel the same way he does. It's just that he's got this thing about being honest with himself. He claims that if a man isn't honest with himself he's going to find it awfully hard being honest about what he does. Including painting. Maybe, deep down he doesn't really care whether he ever becomes a big shot painter or not. Just as long as it's fun and he knows he's doing the best job he can. Maybe—" I halted and stared hard at the ghost. "Is there something wrong, Malcolm? You don't look well."

"Eh? Och, nothing. Nothing at all, lad." He moved over to the window and I noticed that all of the swagger had gone from his step. His shoulders under his velvet jacket were slumped and his face had an old tiredness to it. It was the first time I had ever seen him look his age.

"Jasper?" he said after a long silence.

"Yes?"

"It's plain, is it no', that I will never change?" His voice was as tired as his face and he did not look at me. "I see now that I am as much the vain braggart at this moment in Litchville that I was the day old Calum Carnoustie laid his curse on me back in Gilnochie."

"But—"

"No, Jasper," he said quietly, "it is no use. It is quite clear that there is no hope for me at all, at all. For how can I ever lift the curse when at heart I cannot change my ways? All along I have been telling you, aye and myself, that I was only minding to help your father. Yet all the time the real reason, the *only* reason was to have people think how clever I was! To have people talk about Malcolm MacDhu and say what a grand painter the same one was!"

"But you are a grand painter, Malcolm. You weren't lying about it. You only told the truth about yourself."

He smiled bleakly. "About myself, Jasper. But not *to* myself. There is a big difference. It was only when you told me about your father a few moments ago, and the honesty of the man, that I realized how little the word had ever meant to me." He stared off into space. "I'm thinking that despite all my training in London and Paris, and all the fancy airs I give myself and all the honors I won back in Scotland, your father is a finer painter, aye and a finer man, than ever I was. Than ever I could hope to be."

"But Malcolm," I said, "that's not true! I mean about being honest. If you weren't honest you wouldn't be saying the things you're saying now. Yes, and the things you said about being a braggart. Don't you see, Malcolm? Only someone who's *big* could say these things about himself!"

Perhaps he had not heard me. He did not turn and I could see where he was looking now. Off in the distance at what was left of Strowan Castle. "Soon it will all be gone, Jasper. All the rock and the stone—and the memories, and no one will care at all, at all, of what was and will never be again. Memories of the wild skirl of the pipes as they rallied the clansmen to defend yon walls. Memories of the great hall, blazing with lights, and fine ladies curtsying gracefully before their kilted partners. Memories of spitted boars roasting slowly over the fireplace and flushed faces and the sound of proud young men laughing around the table. And now it is all ending, mortar and stone and dreams ground into a fine dust to be blown away by a cold wind.

"There was a lass once, Jasper. Her name was Alison. She had a lover there in Strowan Castle, a wild lad with a quick temper to him. And always when he was out at the gambling and the romancing she would wait quietly for him to come home. See that window in the room just below what's left of the tower? You can just make it out. Well, that was where the lass would sit and wait for him. She had fair hair and her eyes were as blue as the waters of Loch Nairn and her lips were as ripe and as red as the wild strawberries that bloom around Gilnochie in the springtime."

I didn't say anything. I wasn't quite sure there was anything I should say. I could see the window below the tower where Alison had sat and waited for her lover to come home. It was strange, though, why all of a sudden

Malcolm should have started talking about Strowan Castle. I felt, but wasn't sure, that in some manner it was linked with our conversation of a few moments ago. The bitter words that he had spoken about himself had in some way started him thinking about the castle and the days long ago. And of a girl who had sat by a window waiting for her lover.

Malcolm kept staring off in the direction of the castle and I was beginning to think that he had forgotten I was there, when he turned his head slowly and looked at me. "I was wondering, Jasper, if I might ask a favor of you?"

"Of course."

"In a little while Strowan Castle will be gone. I—I had always meant to paint it. Just so men might remember later on how it had looked. With one thing and another I never got to it." His eyes slid away from my face. "Perhaps now you wouldn't mind asking your father to paint it?"

I frowned, surprised both at his embarrassment and at the words he had just spoken. It wasn't like Malcolm to be embarrassed. Still the suggestion was a terrific one. Strowan Castle was a natural and enough of it was still standing to make a fine study. Besides Pop had always been good at that sort of thing. "Gosh, Malcolm!" I enthused, "that's a super idea. Why, I'll bet it will be the greatest picture yet! We can enter it in the big New York Academy show coming up, too! I'll bet that between Pop and you—"

He shook his head. "I am afraid, Jasper, that I—I have ceased to be a ghost painter. It will be your father's picture, and his alone."

I stared. "But he needs you, Malcolm! I mean without you he doesn't stand a chance of winning in New York! Not a chance! Boy, will everybody around Litchville be let down if that happens! They think right now Pop's the greatest."

Malcolm smiled. "So do I. But for a different reason. And don't you worry, lad. If your father's painting is no' a winning one at least it will be an honest one."

"Sure," I agreed uncertainly.

"Good," said Malcolm briskly. He wheeled around and frowned out of the window towards the castle. "And tell him to hurry, please, before all those labor saving things get there first!"

CHAPTER THIRTEEN

For the last few weeks Pop had been painting mostly what they call still lifes, things like apples and grapes. The other day for a switch he painted cows browsing in a pasture but I guess you could even call *that* still life too. Anyway, I was a little afraid he mightn't go for the idea of painting Strowan Castle. Of course I didn't tell him it was Malcolm's idea. Nor did I mention anything about the old battles that had raged around the walls and the dances and the other things that Malcolm had told me. I just said that soon Strowan Castle would be gone and if it wasn't painted now, it never would be painted. Not that it really made an awful lot of difference, I went on, as he could always paint the twenty story high rise instead. I mean Strowan Castle didn't have a kidney-shaped Hollywood pool nor His and Her garages and a doorman with a silk hat and lots of exciting things like that. It was around this point, as I remember it, that Pop abruptly wiped his palette knife on a rag, shrugged, and said maybe he'd stroll over and take a look at the castle anyway.

At first he had been a little lukewarm about the project. I guess he kind of missed the apples and the grapes. After a couple of days, though, he seemed to get more and more excited. As a matter of fact, I'd never seen him so hepped up about any painting he'd ever done before. Every moment he could spare found him seated before his easel a short way from the castle. Of course he couldn't get it all on his canvas because the whole right wing had already been torn down. He had to work fast with what was left, just as Malcolm had warned the other day. In fact, it became something of a race between the wreckers and Pop to see who would finish first. In a way it was a crazy kind of race at that, as all the wreckers wanted to do was to pull the building down and all Pop wanted was to keep it up long enough to get it down on his canvas.

Pop was happy too, about something else. For the first time in months he couldn't find any evidence that anyone was fooling with the painting. I didn't tell him that Malcolm had promised never to touch his paintings again. First of all, every time anyone mentioned anything about the ghost, Pop would remember all the kidding he had taken, and get awfully mad. And when a painter gets mad he can't paint. Secondly, I figured that the less said about what had been going on before, the better. Pop would be on his own in the biggest show of them all—the New York Academy Exhibition. I didn't want anything to get in the way of what he was doing. That was the reason I didn't go near him when he was working on his canvas. I didn't want to take his mind off his work.

"How is it coming along, Daddy?" Debbie asked one morning while we were having breakfast.

Pop grinned. I hadn't seen him grin quite so broadly in a long time. He seemed his old self again after all the hullabaloo of the past few weeks. "Terrific! I'm really very happy with the way it's coming along, Debbie. You know, it's funny. All my life I've been walking past Strowan Castle yet somehow it seems that I've only gotten to know it in the last week. I don't know what it is but there's something about that old crumbling heap of rock and mortar that really got me. Maybe it's the fact that once it's gone, it's gone forever. Maybe it's something else, something I find difficult to explain. Whatever it is, I could feel it as I worked." He buttered his toast and looked down thoughtfully at his coffee. "Strowan Castle. I'll bet that old pile has seen an awful lot of history."

Mom passed me my cereal. "Judging from the way you've been going you should have it ready for the New York Academy next week."

"Right," Pop said. He stirred his coffee. "I'm afraid, though, that this time I'm not going to win anything."

"Daddy!" exclaimed Debbie indignantly, "don't talk

like that! Just because it's New York! You're still the same painter you've always been."

Pop grinned again. "That's what I mean, Debbie. I've got a hunch from the way things have been going that the painting I submit is going to be an original Henry Trimble, for the first time in months."

Debbie shook her head in dismay. "Daddy, how can you talk like that? What would Albert and everyone else in Litchville say if they could hear you? Why Mr. Pottenbaugh was saying just the other day at the Young Peoples' Fellowship that all Litchville was counting on you! He said you were the greatest New England painter since John Singleton Copley. He also said he personally was going to be—"

"Leaning heavily on me!" Pop interrupted. He took a swig of his coffee and pointed his toast at Debbie across the table. "Look, girl, I'm sick and tired of George Pottenbaugh and everybody else around Litchville leaning heavily on me! Let them lean on themselves for a change! And it isn't John Singleton Copley who's painting Strowan Castle, it's Henry, no-middle-initial Trimble, and if what he submits for the New York Academy isn't good enough, it's too darn bad!"

I guess, looking back again, it was just about Pop's finest hour. If he didn't win anything next week a lot of people around the village were going to be sore at him and feel that he had let them down, but Pop couldn't have cared less. Just as long as he didn't let himself down. Maybe it all comes from the stubborn streak that Mom says all New Englanders have in them and that makes them act different from people in places like France or Japan or Texas.

I think it was the first picture that Pop ever had completed away from the atelier. Maybe, remembering what had happened before, he just didn't want to leave it around where somebody might tamper with it. He had a small room at school where he sometimes did a little work after classes and it wasn't until one night just before the exhibition that he brought the finished painting home. Albert Hooplewaite was with us, and Debbie and Mom. We all crowded around Pop as he carefully removed the wrappings from the canvas and propped it up on the easel.

"There!" he exclaimed, as he stepped back, "Strowan Castle!"

The painting was a pretty big one, about four feet by five. It was a scene of approaching night and there was a lot of deep shadow in it although some thin streaks of light still lingered in the sky. In the gathering darkness you could just make out the lines of the old castle. I'm not too sharp on this art business but I figured the night coming on and swallowing up Strowan Castle was a symbol of something or other. All artists have this thing about symbols. No painting is ever complete without a couple of them in it. If your painting doesn't have even one symbol in it, you're dead.

There was something else about this painting, though, something I hadn't noticed at first glance. From a window just below the darkened tower came a small square of yellow light. It framed the head of a young woman with fair hair. Her eyes were fixed on the road leading up to the castle as if she was waiting for someone. Only then, as my gaze followed hers did I spot him. He was young and he wore a kilt and he seemed to be striding out of the shadows as he made his way towards the castle and the girl at the lighted window.

I stared. There was only one person on earth who walked quite like that, shoulders back, kilt swinging. Only one person who held his proud head so, who wore his Balmoral bonnet at such a rakish angle.

"Malcolm!" I whispered. "It's Malcolm!"

Pop frowned. "Malcolm?"

"The ghost. *Our* ghost. You know, the one I told you about." I gazed at Pop. My skin felt cold. "You never saw him. How could you know what he looked like?"

Pop laughed and ruffled my hair. "You and that crazy ghost of yours, Jasper! Still on your mind, eh?" He tilted his head and examined his painting again. "As a matter of fact, the idea of the girl at the lighted window and the young man coming home in the dusk of late evening was an afterthought. It seemed to explain what the painting was all about. The triumph of light over darkness. Love—" He moved his shoulders in a shrug.

"Love," Albert intoned gloomily, "is an expression of middle class attitudes, Mr. Trimble. Modern day sociologists are only now realizing its multi-dimensional aspects and its capacity to inflict traumatic wounds to the psychic body—"

I didn't wait for the rest. I was already on my way upstairs. Malcolm! He must be the first to know! How had it happened? Pop had never seen Malcolm. How had he known how he looked? Even the kilt in the picture had been the same light-colored red and green tartan of the clan MacDhu. It didn't make sense, but surely Malcolm would know. Malcolm—

I stopped short on the threshold of the room next to the atelier. Malcolm's room. It was empty. Still that could mean nothing. No doubt Malcolm was just saving his ectoplasm. I smiled. "Malcolm? Are you there, Malcolm?"

Nothing stirred. I glanced at the rocking chair by the window. Malcolm's chair. It was motionless. My eyes moved around the small room. "Malcolm?" I said again, only a little louder this time. Again there was no answer.

I hesitated. Malcolm had always been there before when I called. It was strange he wasn't there now. Suddenly I remembered the atelier. Of course! Why hadn't I thought of it before? I poked my head in. It was empty.

"Malcolm?" I inquired again. I peered behind Pop's easel. Just in case Malcolm was playing some game with me. "Are you there, Malcolm?"

I went back to the room next door. Something was wrong. Terribly wrong. Malcolm had always been there before. Only he wasn't there now. I glanced around uneasily. "Mal—" I began, before my eyes fell on the small square of paper lying on the desk near the window. I walked over slowly and picked up the paper and saw there was a message of some kind on it. The handwriting was a thin, spidery scrawl and the letters were formed in an odd, flowery way but I could still read it.

When you get this letter, Jasper, I will be gone.

I cannot say how it has happened but it seems that the curse of old Calum Carnoustie was lifted after I repented my sin of pride to you the other day.

So I am going home, Jasper. After two hundred and fifty years, going home. Already, as I sit here by the window I can hear, far off in the distance, the skirl of the MacDhu pipes, rising and falling, rising and falling like the sough of the wind threshing among the pine trees in the glen beyond Loch Nairn.

She will be waiting there too, the girl I told you of, with the fair hair and the lips as red and as ripe as the wild strawberries that bloom around Gilnochie in the springtime.

116

Farewell, then, Jasper. You are a grand lad with much goodness in you and I will be forever grateful to you for all that you did for a poor homeless ghost.

And now I must go. The sound of the pipes is louder in my ears, and more insistent. I can see faces now too, the faces of my father and of Alison, who waited at the window. They are smiling at me and calling me and I must hasten.

Ever your friend,
Malcolm MacDhu of Gilnochie

I put the letter in my pocket and turned around. As I did so, my elbow brushed against the chair and it started to rock gently just as so often it did when Malcolm was around.

It was still rocking when I closed the door behind me and joined the others downstairs.